Time stood still as his eyes searched hers

In one sweet movement Carlos's lips sought hers, and Vinny gave herself up to the swooning pleasure his touch brought to her hungry body. There seemed to be no end to their kiss or the swelling of their mutual needs and emotions.

Vinny was at once drawn to him and resistant to the power that compelled her. She tried to turn her head away, to hide her lips from his, but even when Carlos released her she felt bound by the very closeness of his body; the scent of his clothes, his skin; the warmth that emanated from him, wrapping them close together, as though in actual bonds.

Moonlight Enough

Sandra Clark

Harlequin Books

TORONTO • NEW YORK • LOS ANGELES • LONDON
AMSTERDAM • PARIS • SYDNEY • HAMBURG
STOCKHOLM • ATHENS • TOKYO • MILAN

Original hardcover edition published in 1982
by Mills & Boon Limited

ISBN 0-373-02533-5

Harlequin Romance first edition March 1983

CHAPTER ONE

HOUR after hour the train had traversed the high plateau of central Spain with only the occasional olive grove to mock Vinny's memories of the very English elms of her father's North-Country estate.

Most of her companions in the first class compartment were still asleep and she watched with eyes that occasionally filled with tears the eternally unfolding landscape. The only break in her reverie came when the guard slid open the doors of the compartment in order to check everybody's tickets.

In correct though halting Spanish she asked him how long now before they reached their destination.

'Granada? *Dos horas*,' he replied briefly.

Thank goodness for that, breathed Vinny to herself when he had gone. She had thought it would be fun to fly part of the way to Granada, stopping off in Madrid to take in some of the sights, and then catch a train for the rest of the journey to Andalucia. That way she would get a chance to see something of the countryside before term started. She knew there would be little opportunity once she started her new job to go sightseeing.

But it had been a long and tiring fifteen hours, with nothing much to do once she had exchanged her few words of Spanish with her fellow passengers, and now she would be pleased to reach journey's end.

She allowed herself to drift back into a dreamy semi-conscious state in which the figure of Zak seemed to loom too prominently for her peace of mind.

It was all due to the book, wasn't it? Her present gloom.

She let her fingers smooth the cover of the slim volume on her lap. It was a book *he* had left behind. Not a parting gift. Nothing like that. Zak didn't believe in that sort of thing—parting, or perhaps especially, gifts. He had simply shed the book as he seemed to shed all his personal possessions and attachments when they were no longer of any use to him. It had just happened that it fell into her keeping. And she had brought it with her, for something to read on the journey.

> *'Twenty-one times have these eyes beheld the changing scene. . . .'*

She paused and recalled the rest of it without even looking down at the page.

> *'I have had enough of moonlight. Ask no more!*
> *Only listen to the voice of pine and cedar*
> *When no wind stirs.'*

Well, there was no pine or cedar, but the sentiment was apt.

With her eyes of deep Atlantic blue and her long, straight ash-blonde hair, she looked very English, very cool and self-possessed, against the dark Latin looks of her travelling companions. Now her blue eyes were even darker with the sudden shadow of some remembered pain. She had let her imagination take hold, with the result that here she was, sitting in a Spanish train, almost crying for a love affair that had never really happened.

Surreptitiously she scrubbed again at a little tear in the corner of one eye. Strange, she mused, she had somehow or other allowed herself to be taken in completely by Zak. Or at least, that was what her parents thought. But were they right? Had she really been duped by his sweet, little-boy manner, his half-spoken promises, his declarations of a love not quite voiced, his hints of romantic possibilities and vague endearments?

And what was she to make of his expectation that she would still be waiting for him, after the summer, when he finally decided to return from Italy?

After the summer? She shuddered at the thought. Her mind flew back to the day when her misgivings had been given something tangible to work on.

They had been lying down, his head innocently on her breast, his eyes closed tight, a half-smile of contentment on his face. It was mid-afternoon, and they were in his shabby little rooms in town, because it seemed more sensible to meet away from the house for a time, and Lavinia had been able to combine her visit with an errand in town for her mother.

It was raining. The sound of the separate drops drumming against the glass seemed to lock them in a world of special intimacy, and Lavinia lay there for quite a while in a cocoon of warmth, waiting for Zak to say something to show that he too felt the same way.

In his rather threadbare maroon velvet trousers

and a floppy-sleeved white shirt he looked like a poet and lay as still as someone posing for a portrait. Even when she kissed him he didn't move. He merely stirred slightly, as if distracted by some minor irritation, so that, stung by his apparent indifference, she had kissed him more urgently, a touch of anger at his composure hardening her lips and bringing with it a sudden wicked urge to bite hard into that soft, curving boy's mouth which seemed so unawakened to her charms.

He had turned his head away and when she had tried, as a last resort, to get him to talk, he had shushed her by placing two fingers on her lips.

'Listen!' he chided. Earlier he had put on a new recording of some medieval instrumental music and its melancholy tones filled the room with what Lavinia would at some other time have thought of as a romantically yearning counterpart to their mood.

Now, however, she was irritated by Zak's obliviousness to her needs. Couldn't he see that she wanted some definite commitment from him? Couldn't he understand that if she had to face a lot of antagonism at home, even to the extent of having to meet him in semi-secret, as now, that he should at least give some outward sign of his caring?

For the first time she began to feel that it was she who was an embellishment to the music—not vice versa as she had always thought. It wasn't the music that was a background to their romance, but the romance which was a background to the music.

She said all this in a rush of angry words, scrambling to her knees so abruptly that Zak fell sideways, hitting his head lightly on the leg of the piano. His face for a moment hardened with irritation, then the old charming smile chased away the shadows and he raised himself on to the pillows scattered around them to get a proper look at her flushed face.

'You look so lovely,' he told her, ignoring what she had said as usual. 'I love it when your eyes flash like that. You usually look so cool and collected.' He pulled her towards him and traced the line of her cheek with the tip of one finger. 'You're my Botticelli angel. When I go to Italy I'm not going to be able to forget you for a minute.'

'*When* you go,' she said drily, then her breath had been stopped by the look on his face. For a moment the fact that once again he had managed to sidestep what she had just said to him was erased from her mind. 'When? . . . Do you mean—when you *go*?'

'It won't be for ages yet,' he said, sinking back among the cushions and closing his eyes once again. 'Not until the week after next, or the one after that. You know I'm always rather vague about dates and things.'

'But you didn't tell me,' she cried accusingly.

'I'm sure I must have,' he said, 'surely?'

'You did not!' she cut in heatedly.

'Perhaps not, then,' he answered infuriatingly. 'It must have slipped my memory. I've really only just made up my mind.'

For a moment or two she sat there, anger and disappointment struggling for supremacy within her. How could he not have told her he was going away? And why wasn't she being asked to go with him?

She remembered how she had put two trembling hands to her cheeks. There was a dreadful feeling of tightness in her throat as if she was going to cry. But she was damned if she was going to cry in front of him, lying there so languidly and doing nothing but smile dopily at her as if everything was all right.

She gave him a hard stare.

'So,' she said at last with a toss of her head, 'you're going to Italy. How nice for you. Do have a good time.'

She wanted to ask him a million questions. How long was he going for, who was he going with—but she held them in check. If he was going to clam up like this then he could jolly well keep his secrets.

Suddenly hurried, she rose to her feet. 'I've just remembered, I've got to go.'

Zak waited until the consort of viols brought the piece to an end and only when the last note had died away did he open his eyes again. By then she was standing over him, shoulders squared, eyes cold.

'I didn't think you'd have to go just yet—you haven't heard the other side of the recording.'

He put out a hand as if to pull her down beside him again, but she brushed his hand aside with unaccustomed brusqueness and turned towards the door. She was wearing the long cotton dress with the little sprigs of green roses all over it that he had said he adored her in, and he caught hold of it by the hem as she turned on her heel.

'You can't go yet,' he said with a teasing smile.

'Can't I?' She tried to tug her skirt free, but he wouldn't let go.

'I'm not ready for you to go yet,' he told her in his winsome little-boy voice.

'Ready? *You're* not ready?' Her voice was tight with anger. 'When will you be ready? When you've had another hour's sleep on my shoulder? What do you think I am? Here!' she had kicked one of the cushions towards him, 'sleep on that. It won't complain.'

With that she had given a hard tug, got her skirt free, and walked rapidly towards the door.

When she turned, she half hoped he would have followed or at least said something in an attempt to restrain her, but he had already sunk back on to the pillows with a childish pout and his face was already composing itself for listening again.

'Goodbye, then,' she had said in a voice which sounded strained and high to her own ears.

And she had gone out, closing the door carefully behind her so as not to betray the depth of her anger.

By the time she had driven the Range Rover all the way home along the side roads, she had worked herself into a fine old temper. So Zak was not only going to *act* as if he was a million miles away, listening to his crumhorns and sackbuts, he was really going to *be* a million miles away, and no further thought about her!

She slammed the car into second gear to get it up the steep incline that led up to the house. The old place had been at its finest at that time of year, the formal rose garden making a glorious blaze of colour against the weathered grey stone at the front of the building. But Vinny saw none of this. Her eyes flashed fire. 'I must have been mad to think that a boy like that knows what love is. Maybe *I* don't know either. But I jolly well know what it's not, and it's not this lack of sharing, this utter nothingness!'

She parked the Range Rover in the stable yard and strode angrily through into the kitchen, flinging down her car keys on to the scrubbed table with such force that Mrs Lax the housekeeper straightened up in alarm. But without a word Vinny had swept on into the study, such an air of her old self about her that her mother had looked up from the household accounts in astonishment.

'Where are all the maps?' demanded Vinny rhetorically with only a cursory word of greeting, and within a few moments she was marching out of the study again, her arms choc-a-bloc with route maps and Michelin guidebooks.

As soon as she was inside her room, she tore off her long cotton dress which she had worn almost constantly since Zak had told her how like the Lady of Shalott she looked, with her filmy, floaty full-length skirts and her ash-blonde hair flowing loosely over her shoulders.

Then she had scrambled into a pair of figure-hugging blue jeans. It was with particular satisfaction that she had threaded a big leather belt through the loops, and when she pulled the buckle tight she did it with an air of totally satisfying defiance. Then she began to spread the maps out on the floor around her. 'That,' she said to no one in particular, 'was positively the last straw!'

Now the Spanish train was at long last pulling into the main station of Granada.

Vinny stretched wearily. Her first wish when she arrived at the villa would be to have a good hot shower and a change of clothes.

She stood up briskly. The past was forgotten now and though tired out after long hours in the train she was all eagerness to get her first glimpse of the city which was to be her home for the next three months.

She watched her fellow passengers climbing down on to the rail tracks to get to the exit on the opposite platform, and, gripping her red suitcase in one hand, her train ticket and new leather bag in the other, she leaped eagerly down to follow them.

Suddenly a grip like a vice almost yanked her arm out of its socket and she was all but knocked off her feet as someone dragged her across the line to the platform on the other side.

Somewhere in the background she had an indistinct impression of a woman's scream and blur of men's voices shouting something she could not understand.

Then she was being hauled bodily up on to the platform, her bag falling open and its contents showering wildly all over the track. Somehow or other her suitcase remained miraculously glued to her hands. She had felt a glancing blow on the side of her shoulder and when she managed to collect her thoughts and arrange events in some sort of sequence she turned angrily on the man who was even now holding her by the arm with such force the pain was bringing tears to her eyes.

For a moment she forgot she was in another country and she broke forth in a torrent of English, demanding to know what the hell he thought he

was doing, pushing her around like this, making
her scatter her personal belongings all over the line
in such disarray, and holding on to her in such a
bullying manner. Didn't he even know the elements
of good manners? She had a good mind to report
him for assault!

Throughout all this the man stood looking down
at her without a word. Then slowly he began to
remove his fingers from their tight hold on her arm.
He was tall and very elegantly dressed from head
to foot in black.

Now he was regarding her flushed-faced outburst with scornful detachment, from between dark
slitted lids, as if totally unmoved by the gathering
of an excited crowd which the vehemence of her
words seemed to have brought to the scene.

She paused in her tirade for a moment, realising
belatedly that he had probably not understood a
word of what she had been saying, and she began to
search frantically for some suitable words in the un-
familiar language with which to extricate herself.

Slowly he brushed some imaginary dust off his
coat sleeve.

'And they tell me the English never lose their
cool!' he said in an impeccable accent.

He looked down at her with a sardonic half-smile
on his face. Then, taking her forcibly by the shoulders, he turned her round to look back across the
track to where her things still lay scattered. Only
now, instead of the empty track, there was an electric train silently snaking along the rails—its heavy
metal wheels cutting through the good leather of
her handbag as if it had been silk.

'Oh, no!' For a moment everything blurred, her

knees began to give way, and she felt someone catch her in strong arms as she started to fall.

When she came round, her face was pressed up against the dark cloth of the man's jacket and she lay there, trembling, with the rough cloth pressing into her cheek. In a moment, though, she regained control and lifted her eyes to his.

Horror, shame, gratitude and humiliation struggled to express themselves all at once. For a moment she could only lean weakly against him, no words able to shape themselves.

Now the distant cries of the other passengers made sense. The sudden painful blow on her shoulder made sense. The brutal grip in which the man had held her—all of it made sense.

Weakly she tried to frame words of thanks, but still nothing would come.

'Better your papers scattered in such disarray than yourself,' he told her sardonically.

Vinny felt her body begin to shake uncontrollably. 'I didn't even hear the train coming up,' she said faintly, pushing a trembling hand across her forehead. 'I just didn't hear it.'

'You look as if you could do with a good stiff drink. Stay here one moment.'

He waited for the train to go by, then, looking both ways along the track, he jumped down and went back to pick up her things. There was lipstick, keys, phrase book, passport, diary, the remains of her make-up bag and—she blushed—a spare pair of disposable panties which she hadn't got around to wearing.

Silently he stuffed them all back in the now rather sorry-looking leather bag and handed it all back to her.

'The bag, I'm afraid, is somewhat *kaput*,' he told her. 'But it seems to me you can light a candle to someone for this escape. Come.'

It was issued as an order and she willingly complied. The crowd at once began to disperse with much shaking of heads and one or two nods of approval bestowed in the direction of Vinny's rescuer. He shrugged these off and led Vinny by the arm towards the station buffet. She winced as he touched her shoulder where the train had glanced off her, but she managed to bite back the cry of pain which rose automatically to her lips. In a moment they were sitting opposite each other at a marble-topped table for two in a corner of the crowded buffet. He pushed a cognac towards her and watched her sip it. At once a rush of fire came into her veins and she managed a wan smile. His answering glance however was grim.

Feeling an eagerness to make amends for the man's evident displeasure, she said, 'I'm sorry I sort of bawled you out like that just now.'

He inclined his head a little.

'It was quite understandable. You looked as if you were sleepwalking. Are you always so dreamy?'

She flushed with annoyance. Although her hands were still trembling, now that she was beginning to recover her composure a little the man's evident disdain for her was beginning to rankle. She regarded him carefully over the table. His Spanish good looks left her cold, she told herself. They seemed to come straight out of a travel brochure— olive tan, flashing black eyes, high cheekbones, haughty turn to the head, proud, straight nose, teeth which flashed briefly and so dazzlingly that she could do nothing for a moment but stare at him as if waiting for the next smile to illumine the beautiful arrogance of his expression.

He wasn't at present in the smiling game, however. His face, now that it seemed clear she was all in one piece both mentally and physically, wore an expression of unmitigated disdain.

'As soon as you've regained some colour I shall have to leave you. I'm already late for my appointment.'

Before she could interrupt to tell him that she was quite all right he said bluntly: 'Are you always as pale as this?'

'I don't know,' she replied rather sharply. 'I can't see myself.'

'You look washed out.' He allowed his eyes to travel expressionlessly over her body, over the grubby T-shirt, the rather tatty-looking jeans, down to her feet in their dirty open-toed sandals.

She blushed unaccountably. If anyone was justified in looking grubby, she was, she thought with a fierce little lift to her chin.

'I've just travelled all the way from Madrid,' she explained lamely after a rather heavy silence during which the man had regarded her with insulting detachment.

'So I surmised,' he replied drily. 'That happened to be the Madrid *rápido* you arrived on. Most tourists like you come that way. It's cheap if not fast.'

She couldn't be sure whether there was some jibe intended or not. Judging by the elegance of his appearance, his self-assurance, he looked like a man used to having people do as he said, and therefore, by implication, used to the power that money might bring. But she couldn't let the assumption that she was just another tourist doing Spain on the cheap pass without comment. She drew herself up in the hard-backed wooden chair and raised her clear blue eyes unflinchingly to his.

'I happen to be working in Granada, actually,' she informed him.   'I'm no tourist just passing through.'

She turned away in order to gather her things together. The man hadn't replied at once, but when she had gathered everything up and was just about to get to her feet, he put out a hand and held her by the forearm with a grip that was only just the right side of good manners.

There was no expression of concern in his voice when he said: 'Are you really sure you're all right now?' She saw his eyes flicker over her face as if assessing it for signs of imminent collapse. 'I think perhaps I should call a taxi for you. Sit down.'

She hesitated. There was no note of concern in his voice. Rather, it seemed as if he would merely be unable to forgive himself for some breach of etiquette if he allowed her to leave before she was fully recovered.

'I'm quite all right now, thank you,' she replied, irked by his order to sit, which was delivered in a tone of voice implying that she had no choice but to do as he commanded. She moved away deliberately, but then was all at once stung by remorse.

He had saved her life. She shouldn't let the man's evident arrogance make her forget those very elements of good manners which she had accused him of lacking in so marked degree.

She smiled rather stiffly, but faltered at the lack of any apparent response in the cool gaze of the man's dark, almost black eyes.

'It's difficult to know how to express my thanks adequately,' she said.

The man seemed unperturbed by her confusion. It seemed even that a slight glimmer of amusement appeared somewhere in the depths of those hypnotically dark eyes.

'One never knows,' he replied softly. 'Fate often finds a way of allowing us to repay old debts.'

Something in the intensity of the man's gaze made her shiver inwardly, but his smile flashed, briefly dazzling her, and an almost roguish gleam lurked in his eyes. For a moment she could not tear her glance from his. The austere lines, the harshness of his expression, were softened, giving him an air of vulnerability.

Hurriedly, with the realisation that she was simply standing almost goggling at him, she began to move away.

Still smiling softly he said: *'Hasta la vista,'* then he settled back to give her an up-and-down look which seemed to take in every aspect of her body. He made no attempt to conceal the nature of his appraisal and Vinny felt herself colour violently. But before she could put him in his place everything around her seemed to go blurry and she felt herself beginning to sway, so that she had to clutch the edge of the table with both hands to stop herself from keeling over. Once again her bag dropped from her grasp, scattering its contents all over the floor, and she felt rather than saw the man's lean brown hands shoot out to catch her.

CHAPTER TWO

Now he was towering over her, pushing her head down between her knees, peremptorily telling her to keep still and be quiet.

She had an impression of his firm, warm hand on the skin underneath her T-shirt at the back of her neck, but though she struggled halfheartedly, he made sure she kept her head down until he was satisfied that the colour was beginning to seep back into her face.

At last he was convinced that she was properly conscious, and only then did his grip slacken and with a small smile of reproof he allowed her to raise her head.

'I shall get you a taxi and take you to your hotel,' he told her in a voice which would brook no further argument. 'Wait here for a minute or two. Will you be all right now?'

Weakly Vinny moved her head in affirmation. From somewhere or other he seemed to spirit another drink and insisted on standing over her until she shakily raised it to her lips.

'I trust you not to move until I get back,' he told her sternly.

She was now in no mood to argue, though she made a feeble gesture as if to go with him.

'There may be a queue at the taxi rank,' he told

her, pushing her back firmly in the chair. 'I'll get one of the drivers to come round to the side exit. Now sit still until I return.'

With that he was gone.

Vinny leaned her head in her cupped hands and tried to steady her breathing. Both the blow to her now throbbing shoulder and the rigours of the long journey, not to mention the emotional shock of realising how close to death or at the very least serious injury she had been, were enough to make her feel faint, but there was also something else, something that made her feel quite shaky and unreal. It was difficult to take in all at once. She felt baffled and confused.

Naturally, she told herself, things seemed strange and confused—to be so far from home, to be so far from the boy she was in love with. And she wasn't used to being organised in this peremptory manner. Her thoughts flew to Zak. He would never order her about like this. No, he was all gentleness and soft persuasion. She shuddered. Life seemed intolerably bleak without him. Yet was it really love? She sipped her brandy with a thoughtful frown. He was so entertaining, so knowledgeable about all kinds of things—about paintings, and books, and music. He was the perfect companion. So why these misgivings?

One thing to his credit, she mused, he never made any undue demands on her. Not like most of the men who came to her father's house, given half a chance. And not like her mysterious rescuer either, she made a guess. She could imagine the sort of demands he would make, given the opportunity. Just one look at those darkly mocking eyes gave his game away. She shivered. He reminded her of a lithe and dangerous wildcat, whereas Zak was by comparison a fireside tabby.

She smiled to herself. She felt safe with Zak. And that was what she wanted, wasn't it? Did it really matter that she sometimes got the niggling feeling that despite the fact that she seemed to have allowed him to take over her entire life, when it came to getting him to make some sort of reciprocal commitment, nothing at all was forthcoming?

She rested her burning forehead on the cool surface of the marble table top, unaware of the curious glances of the passersby.

'Zak!' she sighed. One day, she remembered, she had asked, '*Are* we close? Sometimes I feel that you're a million miles away.'

She hadn't been able to tell him how she yearned for some sign that the feeling he seemed to arouse in her was reciprocated. But he seemed quite content to let things jog along as they were, confident, it seemed, that things would continue in the way that seemed to suit him best. *He* was happy, it seemed, and it apparently didn't occur to him that Vinny was plagued by doubt.

She remembered when she had tried to put into words the feelings that had been bothering her for weeks. Zak had been lying childlike with his head in the crook of her arm, his eyes closed, heavy lashes soft as down on his cheeks. When she had haltingly tried to explain her misgivings, he had for a long time kept silent. She began to wonder if he was asleep, his breathing was so deep and slow and relaxed. But when she had kissed him on the brow as one kisses a sleeping child, he had slowly and with that bewitching cherubic smile, opened his eyes.

'I do love you, Lavinia,' he said simply. Then he had closed his eyes once more.

She had kissed him again, for some unaccountable reason feeling hot tears springing from her eyes. Hastily she had blinked and hidden her face in his curling hair.

Eventually she had been able to bring herself to frame the words.

'I can't help believing you, when you're here, and we're in each other's arms,' she had told him. 'But when you leave me I feel empty, as if it's all been a dream of some kind. I feel nothing—just a sort of hollowness inside. It's as if you could just walk away and never ever think of me again.'

'But I've told you I love you,' he replied patiently, without opening his eyes.

'That's not it,' she had faltered. How to explain that words, however pretty, were no longer enough? How to explain that she just didn't *feel* that he really cared one way or the other about her?

She tried to shake him gently to make him pay attention to what she was saying, but when he pulled her down to touch his lips on hers she was lost in the sense of languor which his sleepy kisses seemed to bring. Here, as always, the tentative conversation ended, and when Zak had gone she was again empty and confused by the feelings which he had somehow aroused but not fulfilled.

'What do you want?' he had laughed, some other

time when she had tried to express her bewilderment, 'a wedding ring?'

'Of course not!' she had replied hotly. 'I'm not asking you to marry me.' Her cheeks flamed.

'I'll give you a ring, if that's what you want.' His eyes had observed her narrowly.

For a moment her breath had been stopped. He would marry her? Then he must love her. Despite her continual misgivings.

For an instant she felt an overwhelming joy. To be certain, once and for all, that he was hers and she was his. An end to all doubt. She looked at his beautiful boy's face, his hair tumbling wildly about his head like a faun's, his boy's body which she had never enjoyed, which even now she blushed to imagine as the body of a man.

A dull weight seemed to slow her thoughts. He was a child, and children didn't marry. They might pretend. They might wear flowers in their hair and exchange gilt rings that glinted for a moment like gold in the sunshine of a May morning, but they didn't enter into the serious solemn world of holy vows, to have and to hold from this day forth for evermore. To trap a child in that way would be wrong.

That was when Vinny realised that she could never commit herself to a marriage such as theirs would be. Playing little mother to his boy-child, and trapped, herself, in a children's game, she would inevitably yearn for something else. For a king, perhaps, but not for a boy-prince.

She had felt overwhelmed by a sweet, piercing sorrow, the sorrow that comes with the knowledge that one's childhood has fled, that all things pass.

Even with the knowledge of all this, though, she somehow seemed to lack the will to do more than drift along with a now ever-present sense of unease, a feeling that, whatever her own wishes in the matter, things were obscurely on the verge of change. On the surface things seemed to go on much as usual, though, and to say that she was unaware of her parents' disapproval would have been untrue, yet she gave no more than a passing thought to it until one morning, coming down to breakfast as usual, things finally came out into the open.

Her father, a still active landowner, had already been out to one of the farms, but as usual he was back at the house for breakfast. A handsome grey-haired man in his late fifties, he was reading the *Financial Times* as usual. Vinny's mother, sitting opposite him in her usual place at table, was in the middle of giving some late instructions to one of the housemaids for a little luncheon she was giving that day.

The first sign Vinny had that anything was wrong was when her mother, on seeing her come into the room, at once dismissed Gerde and started to busy herself quite unnecessarily with the coffee.

'Black or white today, Vinny?' she had asked in a casual tone, with only the briefest glance at her husband to see if he had noticed the arrival of his youngest daughter.

'White,' replied Vinny. 'And sugar, please.'

'Given up on the diet already?' her mother had remarked lightly, with an amused look at the trim form of her daughter. She was trying to establish a note of calm before the storm broke, it seemed.

Vinny took her place between her parents.

Carelessly she said, 'Zak says he rather likes plump women——' but she could have bitten off her tongue at once, for Zak's name seemed to have the same effect on her father as one of the cattle prods they sometimes used on the steers at market time. He shot forward in his seat, crumpling his paper to one side. Then he looked searchingly into Vinny's face.

'I've been meaning to have a word with you about him, Vinny.' He paused ominously. 'It seems to me you've been seeing rather a lot of that young man recently.' He paused again as if weighing his words. 'Don't you think it's about time we were all given some inkling of his future plans? He's been out of music college for some time now and there's still no sign of a job in the offing.'

'He doesn't believe in plans,' Vinny started to explain. 'He just wants to make music.'

'Make music——?' Her father gripped his paper with both hands.

'Is he any good, Vinny?' asked her mother gently, her words covering but not obliterating her husband's expostulation of derision. 'Could he get a job in an orchestra? Is that what he wants?' She went on. 'It's high time he started to think seriously of the future. His family are hardly in a position to help out.'

'I shouldn't think there's much demand for lute-nists in orchestras these days,' interrupted her father testily.

'He plays woodwind too,' protested Lavinia mildly.

'Pan-pipes?' The tone was sarcastic.

'Your father means that he seems so ethereal,'

her mother added in an attempt to deflect her husband's unusual acerbity.

'A day out with the Harborough would soon sort him out,' he added testily.

'Hunting's not his scene, and anyway, he is sorted out. He does no harm,' remonstrated Vinny. She remembered now that she had been suddenly close to tears, though she couldn't imagine why.

'He does *you* harm perhaps, have you thought of that?' Her father looked fiercely over the top of his paper. 'You used to be full of the joys of spring, singing like a lark all over the damned show, now you moon about the place like a lost soul. I hardly hear you speak from one day to the next. And you never go anywhere.'

He humphed and hawed and rustled his paper in embarrassment at having to go so unusually far in expressing his true feelings.

'It's certainly true, you have no social life to speak of these days,' interrupted her mother, concern showing briefly in eyes which had been almost as blue as Vinny's own twenty years ago.

'Oh, please, don't be hard on him. We enjoy ourselves listening to music, reading poetry, talking.' Vinny looked perplexed. 'He wants to get a job, but he's not sure what to do yet. He says it's got to be just right. But so far nothing suitable has turned up. And anyway,' she broke out, 'it's so peaceful, being with him. He's so tranquil. It's like——' she stopped. How to tell a bluff old landowner like her father that being with Zak was like being lost in the deep, silent heart of a magical forest?

'You're living in a dream world,' he protested.

'She was always a dreamy child,' remarked her mother innocently.

'Be quiet, Alicia!'

Her mother raised her eyebrows but relapsed into silence.

Vinny, however, was pulled up sharp by the ill-concealed anger in her father's voice. It was so unlike him to speak out in this way to her. Her reverie momentarily shattered, she was provoked to answer in similar vein.

'Why should life be all decisions and ambitions and striving for attainment, for money, status, material goods, high life, all that?'

She faced him squarely, her ash-blonde hair framing a face which was now flushed with hurt anger.

'That's not you talking,' he replied, failing to keep the red of emotion from suffusing his cheeks. 'You know I don't expect you to grow up into a cold-hearted little go-getter . . .' he paused and rustled his paper more violently, 'but what I do expect is that you try to make something of your life. Since you left college you've done nothing but moon around, with no apparent thought for the future. You should be out in the world, not mooning around some squalid student bedsitter every night of the week. I know you don't *need* to get a job——' his tone became conciliatory, but she could tell by the way he hung on to the *Financial Times* that it was only with an almighty effort that he managed to keep a note of reasonableness in his voice, 'but even so,' he went on, 'I think you might try to get involved in something useful for a year or two before you settle down for good.'

'You always did so well at your studies,' broke in her mother. 'Your father expected quite something——'

'It's difficult to get anything interesting these days. The economic situation isn't my fault,' Vinny replied halfheartedly.

'No, my dear,' he replied, 'but you could at least put yourself on the market. You've got a damned good degree, and all for what? To throw away on someone like——' he stopped, thought better of what he had been about to say, then glared straight into her eyes.

She didn't shrink. She had always been a spirited child and now, though she knew it grieved him to see her so apparently lacking in ambition, she was unable to act.

'No one can blame you for not being able to find a job as a linguist here, in the depths of the countryside,' he tried another tack, 'but what's to stop you moving away? You could go anywhere you choose. You know I'll provide an adequate allowance for a little flat in town. I can't see what's stopping you.'

For a moment Lavinia sat with her mouth open like one stunned, before she was stung to reply.

'But I like it here!' she exploded. 'It's my home! You sound as if you're telling me to get out!'

'Perhaps I am!' he replied rather too forcefully, crushing the already crumpled newspaper down on top of his fortunately empty cereal bowl.

'Gregory!' Her mother's sharp interruption could have been at the unusual havoc Vinny's father was wreaking on the once orderly breakfast table, or it could have been at the suggestion that her youngest daughter should be thrown out on to the streets like a homeless waif. Lavinia didn't stop to enquire which. Instead she launched herself into the attack.

'Throw me out? Your own daughter? Are you supposed to be my father?' She turned angry eyes on her mother. 'Did I hear him properly? He wants to throw me out! He's a monster, not a father!'

She had half risen, cheeks flushed, voice raised higher and more spiritedly than of late.

'Ha!' Her father settled back in his chair with an air of triumph, much as he did in the old days when they would both spend hours arguing about all kinds of things and Vinny had been into putting the world to rights.

'Ha!' he said again, more emphatically. 'At least that's got some honest reaction from you. I was beginning to think you'd lost all your spirit.'

He leaned forward and his face was serious. 'Listen to me, my girl. Either you get yourself something sensible to do around here—in which case you can live in the house for as long as you like, or, failing that, you can jolly well take yourself off to somewhere where you can find a sensible occupation. But what I'm not having,' and he looked so stern she knew he meant it, 'is a daughter of mine mooning around all day, wasting her talent and getting under everybody's feet. I hate waste. It's the sheer waste of it all that appals me. Besides——' he settled back, sure now of what he was saying, 'that boy is no good for you, my dear. He'll be asking you to marry him next. *Then* I'd like to see him find a job that suits him. That'd be the day, believe me. He'd be living off you before you could turn around.'

Lavinia sat as if her father had reached forward and slapped her across the face.

'Zak?' she managed to croak when the first effects of her anger and astonishment had subsided. 'How dare you say a thing like that, about Zak? Don't you know him at all? He despises money. He really hates all this——' She waved her arm generally to take in the lovely Georgian house which had been in her family for generations with its rolling parkland stretching to the horizon on all sides.

'He positively hates all this pretentiousness, this show of wealth for its own sake, this——' but she allowed her words to trail off, for her father's expression had taken on a thunderous aspect and for a moment she was truly frightened. Only her mother's restraining hand seemed to calm him, and with a shrug which seemed to express a bravado she did not really feel, Vinny got up from the table and very, very carefully replaced her napkin by the side of her plate without another word.

'Have you had enough already?' her mother asked in an attempt to smooth things over as best she could.

'Quite, thank you,' said Vinny, her face as adamant as her father's. Then she walked calmly from the room without further ado.

To make matters worse, it was only a few days after this that Zak had casually dropped his bombshell about going to Italy. Vinny was confused. On the one hand she was jolly sure she wasn't going to be browbeaten into giving him up just because her father had this bee in his bonnet about him. It was a ridiculous suspicion. And, she thought angrily, he would no doubt say the same about any man she wanted to marry. Most of the men she knew couldn't hope to match up to Daddy's wealth. Tough luck, she thought, he's just going to have to get used to a pauper son-in-law.

On the other hand, she remembered, her thoughts in turmoil, she was blowed if she was going to be kept on ice for anyone, sitting at home throughout the summer while Zak lived it up on the Italian Riviera. All that stuff about museums didn't wash with her, she'd muttered darkly, she knew men.

When Zak turned up then a few days later as if nothing had happened, her heart was clutched with a momentary anguish as she looked into his face. 'He's so sweet and pretty,' she thought, weakening in her resolve for a moment.

His hair was soft and sprang up in little elf curls around his head so that when he gave her his cherubic smile she was almost lost in the piercing sweetness of an undefinable longing. It was only when his expression became a childish scowl as she told him she was too busy to see him that she managed to regain her balance.

'Child!' she responded with unexpected vehemence. 'Sulking like that!'

He looked shocked. 'I'm sad, that's all,' he told her huffily. 'It makes me sad that you won't see me. I leave soon.'

'Yes,' she answered tartly, 'so you do.'

He gave her a sidelong glance. 'I really thought I must have told you I was going away. You're always in my thoughts. It seemed as if I had told you.'

'Well, you didn't. And I don't believe you thought you had either. But it doesn't matter.' She picked out a phrase he himself was always using when he felt the need to detach himself from any responsibility for his actions, 'One does what one must.' It was always his way of saying that if she didn't like what he was doing, that was just her tough luck.

But his answering smile was such that its innocent unwariness pulled at her heartstrings yet again.

'Yes, that's right,' he told her contentedly. 'You're beginning to understand me at last. You see,' he said, taking her by the hand, 'my uncle is driving down to Italy. He always stays with friends near Florence for the summer. This year he thought I might drive down with him. You wouldn't expect me to say no to a free trip, would you?'

Lavinia felt mean. 'Of course not. It's just—it's just that you didn't tell me—and—I don't know when we'll meet again.'

'We'll meet again, don't worry, my sweet. After the summer.' He kissed her, standing under the willow tree near the rose garden. It was a sweet lingering kiss, but cool, like a child's chaste touching of lips. Vinny turned away, confused.

It was somehow not as painful as she had imagined. In fact, she felt something like relief sweep over her. A decision once made was best acted upon at once.

She had made up her mind in a rush. If she was to wash this boy right out of her hair, it was best to do it sooner rather than later. Soon, before his sweet winsomeness had ensnared her heart completely.

'Take care,' she had said, turning briefly back to him with a rueful smile. 'I hope it turns out the way you want.'

He held her close for a moment. 'I know it will,' he said when he released her. 'We will be together again, after the summer, you'll see. I'll bring you lots of postcards of all the paintings I've seen.' He smiled happily. 'I'm really looking forward to it.'

She hadn't been able to answer then. There seemed nothing she could say to a remark like that.

Things had happened quickly after he left. Together with her father's ultimatum and Zak's absorption in his own affairs, there seemed no point in just hanging around all summer, in her father's phrase 'getting under everyone's feet.' And besides, she'd had enough of moonlight, hadn't she?

She had spent some hours browsing through the motorists' guide to Europe and then, almost at random, had applied for a summer job as a teacher of English in a private school in the South of Spain. It was run by a friend of her brother and it was by pure chance she had heard mention of a possible vacancy.

'That's my girl!' said her father with a pleased chuckle when he heard the news.

But her mother had asked, 'It is Italy where Zak is to spend the summer, isn't it, dear?'

Lavinia had laughed almost gaily. 'Honestly, Mummy, do you think I'm quite mad? As if I'd go

chasing after him all that way! It was just a silly
infatuation, that's all. I was under a spell like the
princess in the fairy story. I'm free of all that now.
I can't wait to get out and do something on my
own account.'

If it wasn't strictly true yet, it soon would be,
she vowed, with just the suggestion of a tear in her
eye.

A friend of a friend who had just had a stint at
the School rang her up the night before she left.

'There's skiing only half an hour's drive up into
the Sierra,' he told her. 'And there's a rather re-
markable glacier which is well worth a visit. Oh,
and of course, there's the Alhambra, and a café
that all the students go to called El Suizo, and a
little club down the Calle de las Tablas where you
can hear the best flamenco in all Andalucia—but
Jean will be able to tell you all about that.'

'Jean?' she queried.

'She's the daughter of the family you'll be staying
with.' There was a pause on the other end of the
line. 'Give her my——' There was another pause.
Lavinia thought she heard a deep sigh, but the line
was muzzy with interference of some kind anyway.
'Just mention my name.' He paused again. 'You
won't forget that, will you?'

Vinny gave her reassurances. 'And thanks for
your help,' she finished.

Accommodation had been quickly fixed up
through the friend of her brother in the home of a
British banker and his wife who lived in a large
villa just outside Granada.

She raised her head at last and looked round the
station café. Despite everything she was glad she

had made the effort to come. Soon she would be greeting her hosts and would at last be able to get out of these sticky travel-stained clothes and into something fresh and pretty.

If only the taxi would hurry up!

CHAPTER THREE

IT seemed an age before the man returned, but somehow the thought never once crossed Vinny's mind that he would perhaps remember the urgency of his broken appointment and leave her there until she had recovered sufficiently by herself to call a taxi. She knew, just knew, he wasn't that type, though what type he was she couldn't surmise. It was no surprise, then, when she at last felt a tap on her shoulder and turned, with a tremor of antici-pation, to see his lithe dark frame towering over her.

He drew his lips back in a brief, cold smile.

'I've had the devil's own job to get hold of a taxi, but come, before he's snapped up by someone else.'

He got hold of her red suitcase in his free hand and with the battered bag and its contents tucked under her own arm, she allowed him to lead her through the crowds to a side exit where the taxi was already waiting.

With her luggage on the seat next to the driver and herself safely ensconced in the back, he turned questioningly towards her.

'Well?' She looked at him blankly. He peered closely into her face. 'Are you all right?'

'Yes.' She shivered at the searching look he gave her.

'Well, where to?'

Vinny blinked. There were two lines on either side of his mouth. They seemed to emphasise the clean-cut strength of his jaw.

'Your hotel?' he asked impatiently.

She flushed, and her mind seemed to go blank. In all the confusion her destination had been chased from her thoughts.

'I'm not staying at a hotel,' she managed to say while she tried to collect her thoughts together. 'I'm staying with friends of friends.' Then she turned wide blue eyes beseechingly up to him. 'I'm sorry, I can't remember their address——' A cold fear suddenly gripped her as she desperately sought the name of the villa, or the name of the family with whom she would be staying. Nothing came.

'I'm sorry ——' she faltered. Her mouth went dry. Suddenly she felt very foolish and very, very helpless. She hadn't the courage to look at her rescuer now, dared not outface the contempt she would surely see in his eyes.

She bowed her head. 'I can't remember where I'm staying,' she told him in a small voice like a child confessing some misdemeanour. 'It's gone completely.'

His voice when it came was unexpectedly gentle. 'Take your time,' he told her. 'You've had a bigger shock than you realise. You're bound to be a little confused.' He waited.

'It's no good.' She looked up at him at last, her

blue eyes full of a beseeching humility. 'My mind's a complete blank.'

'You must have written it down somewhere, this address,' he stated practically, giving a brief look at the taxi driver, who was beginning to show signs of impatience.

'Yes,' she brightened, 'in my bag. Of course, I wrote down the address in my book.' Why on earth had she not thought of that at once? Quickly, anxious not to delay the driver any longer, she opened up her handbag and began to search through it. But of her address book there seemed to be no sign. She fumbled through the contents once again. Phrase book, keys, passport, diary, lipstick, a sorry-looking make-up bag, spare panties— but of her address book there was still no sign.

'Oh no!' she groaned, leaning her head back against the seat. All at once a feeling of utter helplessness pervaded her every fibre.

'Don't give up so easily.' The man's tone was matter-of-fact. 'It must have been overlooked when everything fell out. Just go through your bag once again to make certain.'

He made her tip everything out on to the seat, but there was no sign of the book. He said something or other to the driver, who sighed audibly, gave a baleful glance in Vinny's direction, then switched off the engine of his cab and took out a pack of cheap cigarettes.

'I'll have another look on the track. You stay here.'

As he turned to go she put out a hand. 'But what about your appointment?' A worried frown momentarily creased her brow.

'I've already written that off,' he told her. 'This will surely only take a moment or two, however.'

With that he was again plunging off through the crowds on her behalf.

Vinny sat back guiltily and tried to let her anxieties unravel themselves. At least the rain had stopped for a moment. Water still gushed along in the gutters and the sky was overcast. What she could see of Granada was grey. Grey skies, grey buildings, grey streets, even grey pigeons. She half-smiled. It wasn't what she had expected.

This time the man was gone an unconscionably long time and she began to doubt whether he would in fact now return, but at last she saw the tall dark figure threading its way back towards her.

His face was full of concern and his hands, she noticed, were empty.

When he came up to her he scrutinised her face. 'Have you remembered anything?' he asked.

She shook her head, suddenly frightened.

'I too have had no luck,' he told her. 'I even checked with the chief of station, but nothing has been handed over.' Now for the first time she saw something like impatience in his eyes. 'Surely you must know the name at least of these people with whom you are to stay? Who are they? What business perhaps have they in Granada?'

Vinny bit her lip. 'They're just friends of friends. Everything happened so quickly—my deciding to come out here, finding accommodation. I simply put their telegram saying it would be all right to stay with them into my address book at the page where I'd written their address.'

She could have said that her mother's social sec-

retary had dealt with the initial correspondence and
that it had been because her thoughts were almost
totally taken up with Zak in those last few hectic
days that she had scarcely given a thought to her
hosts beyond the fact that they were recommended
by her brother's best friend, had a villa with a pool,
and a daughter named—she prodded her
memory—Jenny, was it? or Jan? Something like
that anyway.

She looked up at the man, whose face was now
stern. She felt suddenly intimidated by him and it
made her speak more aggressively than she
intended. 'You must surely have seen the book
when you picked all the other things up? I can't
imagine why you would leave it behind. Heavens,
it's bright green! No one could miss it.' She made
as if to climb out of the taxi.

'And where do you imagine you're going now?'
he demanded abruptly, barring her way with his
body.

'Obviously I'll have to go and have a proper look
myself,' she glowered.

'I do have eyes in my head,' he told her, equally
irritated. 'Do you think I can't see an address book
lying in front of me?'

'Apparently not,' she retorted, dismissing him
with a toss of her head.

Now her spirits had revived somewhat she was
angry with herself that she had put herself at the
mercy of the man's undoubted inefficiency. He
must have seen the book. It was a bright green, not
easily overlooked. Her words, however, had stung
him. She felt, rather than saw, the muscles of his
body go tense. His jaw was set in an unforgiving

line and his eyes swept coolly over her with none of the sardonic approval in them of only ten minutes ago. He stepped aside to let her get out of the taxi.

'Do you want me to dismiss the driver?' His voice was like ice.

'You may as well,' she replied, climbing out to stand beside him. Gosh, she thought, he's tall. She had to look up into his face. He returned her glance without smiling and added, 'I can't imagine he's pleased at being kept hanging around for nothing.'

The man took this remark with no visible change in his expression. He simply turned to the driver and said something, making as if to reach for his wallet. But the driver raised one hand as if to say thanks for nothing and drove off with a lot of ostentatious over-revving of his engine.

'I can quite see how he feels,' the man remarked in tones of ice.

Vinny tossed her head, then she made as if to pick up her suitcase.

'What's the matter? Don't you trust me?' He took the case from her and put it down again. 'Leave it. You'll see at once that it's not there. I can waste a further five minutes while you look, having already wasted thirty-five.'

Vinny had the grace to blush. It was humiliation that made her speak out angrily, though in self-defence. 'I wouldn't dream of allowing you to waste any time at all, given the choice. As it was entirely your own fault that you got yourself involved in my affairs it seems to me you only have yourself to blame for wasting time.'

She knew it was unfair even as she said it, but

guilt made her unfair. She was unprepared, however, for the man's sudden cold anger. His face became as expressionless as a mask, only his eyes flashed their contempt for her. For a moment she thought he was going to hit her, but instead he stepped back. 'I apologise for pressing my unwelcome attentions upon you. That is not my custom. Please excuse me from all further concern in your affairs.' With a formal inclination of the head, he turned coldly on his heel and started to walk off into the crowd. All at once the stupidity and rank injustice of her remarks became apparent to her.

'Wait! Don't go!' Suddenly it seemed desperately important that he didn't just walk off like that. 'I'm sorry!' she shouted after him. 'Please wait!'

He had heard her cry and paused, half turning back towards her.

'I'm sorry,' she repeated, 'I don't know what made me say that.'

His face still wore a cold, shuttered looked and she had no way of guessing what he was thinking. She felt only the barrier between them, shutting her out. To her horror she felt hot tears begin to course down her cheeks. Swiftly he was beside her, taking her in his arms, holding her tightly to him, his hand, she noticed, in surprise, stroking her hair, lifting her tear-stained face so that she was forced to look straight into his eyes.

'You must be one of the most spoilt, ungrateful as well as stupid girls I've ever come across,' he informed her in measured tones of contempt which were at total variance with the way he still held her.

His scorn wounded her like a whiplash and she was forced to blurt: 'You're not fair!' before he held her at arm's length and laughed softly in such a way that she felt angry all over again. 'Stop laughing at me!' she cried out. 'I've already apologised. What more do you want?'

'Not apologies,' he replied at once. 'Any calculating little fool can apologise when they realise they've overstepped the mark.' He went on holding her, oblivious to the passersby. 'Not only do you bawl me out on the platform as if I was some common pickpocket caught with my hand in your purse, you also accuse me of being blind as well as stupid. I've only done what any other traveller would have done for someone in distress.' He looked mockingly down at her. 'Why anyone let you loose without a chaperone I shall never know.'

'You missed out one thing in your list of things you've done for me,' Vinny told him, trying to step away from him and running nervous fingers through her dishevelled hair.

His lip began to curl as if ready to counter more insults, but she looked up sincerely and innocently into his eyes. For a long moment their eyes seemed to mesh and a shiver ran through her before she managed to say softly, 'You also, as it happens, managed to save my life.'

He shrugged. But his glance had lost its grimness and there was an ironic gleam in his eyes. He seemed to tower over her and she became powerfully aware of the faint tangy scent of his skin and the fine lines at each side of his mouth. His lips parted to reveal perfectly even white teeth in a smile which was totally devastating. She tried to step back, but her limbs didn't seem to be functioning too well. She could only stand as if mesmerised by him. For a moment neither of them uttered a word, then his eyes gleamed devilishly once more.

'I could give you a good spanking.' He continued to smile, despite his words. 'I'm a push-over, it seems—is that the word?—for a little angel like you. Damsel in distress? Perhaps the days of chivalry are not yet over?' He took her arm. 'Let's go and have another look on the track.' He picked up the suitcase in one easy movement and turned back towards the station.

'I don't deserve your help,' she told him, all contrite now.

He merely looked at her with disbelief. 'I'm sure it's out of character for you to humble yourself for anyone. Don't overdo it.' His manner became briskly efficient. 'Come, let's have another look in order to set your mind at rest and revise your opinions about my eyesight, if not my intelligence.'

As he had already told her, there was no sign of the book on the track, and further enquiries at the stationmaster's office failed to produce any response.

'That seems to be that.' He turned to her.

Vinny had been thinking desperately and now she raised her eyes to his. 'If the worst comes to the worst I can always ring up home. My mother's secretary will have a record somewhere of the address. She dealt with all the correspondence. I shall just have to book into a hotel for the night.'

Her words, said so artlessly, seemed to have an electrifying effect on the man and he at once released her arm. For a moment he simply looked at her without speaking.

'Well,' he said at last, 'I can see that now you are yourself again you should have no problems whatsoever.'

Vinny was perplexed by the abrupt change in his manner. Not quite knowing what to make of it she went on, 'Of course, I'd rather try to find them myself. There must be a way of jogging my memory.' She furrowed her brow, but it was impossible. 'If only there was a list of foreign residents, something like that,' she said.

'It would be like looking for a needle in a haystack,' he told her. 'What might help is if you could remember where this man works.'

'He's a banker,' replied Vinny.

The man's face became wooden. 'That is a thread of hope,' he said flatly. 'Can you remember which bank?'

She shook her head.

'You're really hopeless, aren't you?' He sounded exasperated—as well he might, thought Vinny.

'It was a private bank,' she offered tentatively.

'A Spanish one?' he asked.

She nodded. 'I only heard the name once, in passing,' she muttered, shamefaced, bending her head as if trying to hide behind a curtain of silky ash-blonde hair. She peeped a glance up at him, but his expression gave nothing away.

'You're an idiot of the first water.' He took her hand. 'What on earth possessed you to set foot in a foreign country without an army of nursemaids in tow?' He regarded her chastened hanging of the head without pity.

'It's not my fault,' she tried to say. 'It's nothing

to do with me what the man does for a living. I'm only his guest, not his biographer.'

'Not even his guest at this rate,' remarked the Spaniard drily.

'You are infuriating!' glowered Vinny.

'I? Ha!' The man uttered an exclamation of derision. 'Let me remind you, *señorita*, it is not I who wanders lost in the streets of Granada! Come, enough of all this wrangling. Time passes.'

Before she could ask where they were going he had picked up the case once more and taken her by the arm and was briskly leading her out of the station entrance towards the main thoroughfare.

'Where are we going?' she asked breathlessly, trying in vain to pull away from him, but he merely tightened his grip on her arm. She felt an overwhelming urge to run. The power of his muscular frame seemed to overwhelm her and she felt her senses reeling from his proximity so that she almost stumbled again. But he propelled her relentlessly across the road and in a minute or two they were walking briskly down a narrow tree-lined street. When they came to the first hotel with a public bar he pushed her inside and forced her to sit down at a table for two.

'Stay here. I'll go and beg a telephone directory from the manager, then we'll just have to go down the list. Your host is presumably something in the foreign department?'

'I suppose so, yes,' shrugged Vinny, bewildered now by it all. 'I don't really know.'

'I didn't expect you to,' he retorted. 'At least now we are narrowing the field. Five minutes ago we had the whole of Granada to scour. Now we only have the banking fraternity.'

Before she could think of a suitable retort he had left her, and she sank back, pink with humiliation and self-recriminations. Now her shoulder was really beginning to throb and she felt very small and weak and lost. All she wanted was a kind word, but instead she was lumbered with this strange, often hurtful man, who was so bewildering in his rapid changes of mood. She didn't know where she was half the time with him. One minute she would catch a look in his eyes which made her blush with the frankness of its meaning, the next he was all brusque efficiency, sweeping her along as if her wishes were of no consequence, and the next he was coldly aloof as if she was the biggest bore on earth. Which she undoubtedly was.

She was still squirming at the thought when he came back with a directory and two large cups of coffee and a plate of pastries. He cut short her thanks and proceeded to read aloud the list of private banks based in the city. She stopped him after three or four and he repeated the name for her.

'Perhaps ... but I'm not absolutely sure.' She bit her lip.

Without doing more than raise one sardonic eyebrow he read through the rest of the list. Vinny thought one more was a possibility and told him so. She was puzzled by the look on his face as he read. It was like someone who has rediscovered a story from childhood and re-reads it in an attempt to recapture an old, half-forgotten memory of something precious. But once the list was finished he slammed the book shut and rose briskly to his feet. Before she could say anything he was heading for the phone in the lobby.

It seemed an age while she waited for him. Her anxiety grew. She had finished her coffee and was playing with the paper sugar sachet on the edge of her saucer, tearing it up into countless little shreds, when he finally returned. He thrust a piece of paper in front of her on which he had scribbled a name and an address. At once recognition flooded through her. She turned eyes brimming with tears of gratitude on him, but he brushed her thanks aside with a shrug.

'How on earth did you do it?' Her eyes were full of admiration.

'Come,' he was non-committal, 'let's go.' In a moment he had hustled her outside. A taxi pulled up almost at once and she turned to him, suddenly aware that she knew not even his name.

'I have an appointment I cannot miss now,' he told her abruptly. 'Don't let the taxi driver rob you. It shouldn't cost more than a couple of hundred pesetas. And by the way, I can't offer you dinner, but what do you say to lunch tomorrow?'

The taxi driver was already whistling with impatience.

'Yes, yes,' she said, disturbed suddenly by the thought of saying goodbye. Her hands were shaking. 'But it should be I inviting you to lunch—small payment for your help.'

'Nonsense. See me at one o'clock in El Gran Café in the main square. Anyone will tell you where it is.'

'I don't even know your name——' she faltered. But already cars were piling up in the narrow street behind the taxi and the driver was calling out impatiently to them.

'Get in—see me tomorrow.' He paused and smiled briefly. *'Hasta la vista!'* He raised one hand in farewell.

Vinny had to throw herself into the back of the taxi then as the driver, regardless of safety, started to move off. She just had time to turn round and look out through the rear window as they joined the fast-moving stream of cars coursing down the street, but the man had already turned abruptly back into the hotel lobby.

Vinny slumped in her seat and closed her eyes.

What a beginning! And what a fool she had shown herself to be! No wonder he had looked at her with such contempt. She would have to thank him properly when she saw him the next day, but how her faltering words could repay him for the time and trouble and the minor miracle of finding the address like that, she couldn't imagine.

She shuddered, half in fear and half in some as yet unnamed emotion when she recalled the saturnine gleam in his eyes as she had broached the question of thanks in the station buffet. Now there was an even bigger debt to pay, and the devil only knew what price he would want to exact from her.

She shivered again. Really, she must be quite mad to agree to meet him, a perfect stranger, someone who in less dramatic circumstances would be nothing more than a casual pick-up. Daddy would have a fit, she thought, if he knew. She would have to watch her step from now on.

On the other hand, she mused, it was only a lunch date. And in the centre of town. Her thoughts began to slow with fatigue as the taxi laboured up the long winding road above the town. It was with a jolt that she realised they were already pulling into the drive of a gorgeous white-walled villa with a fine view over the city. Scarlet flowers clambered in haphazard profusion over the walls and more flowers hung in curtains of blazing colour from the balconies.

Even before she had climbed stiffly down with her luggage, a man and a woman, unmistakably English despite their deep tans, came on to the drive to greet her.

For the second time that day Vinny became acutely conscious of how travel-stained she must look.

'My poor dear, you must feel absolutely dreadful! Someone explained everything that happened over the phone. Do come in.'

The man took her case, and his wife, her face full of a genuine warmth and concern, took Vinny's arm and led her indoors.

CHAPTER FOUR

VINNY must have been tired out by the events and misadventures of her long journey, for she slept right through until mid-afternoon on the next day. It was with a drowsy sense of disappointment that she looked across at her little red morocco travelling clock and realised that she had missed her lunch date with the Spaniard completely.

Well, she thought sleepily, it couldn't be helped

now. And it was probably for the best. It had been a kind of dangerous idea too, somehow. She could not get out of her mind the way the man had looked at her between the times when he had merely been organising things and acting angry.

For the next day or so she felt no inclination to do anything very much, not even sightseeing, before school started. She felt heavy and drowsy as if under some kind of spell, and the memory of her rescuer slipped to the back of her mind. Only her shoulder, which was still painfully bruised, reminded her sharply, whenever she forgot about it and brushed against something, of her experience on the day she had arrived.

Her room was very pretty, tiled in the Spanish manner, and she had a little wrought-iron balcony which overlooked the garden, and a separate shower room all to herself, done out in green and white Moorish-style ceramics.

As she lay in bed she was, she realised, beginning to feel the first niggling little qualms about starting her new job. It was not only a new job; it was her first real job. But there was nobody she could tell about such misgivings, though the Cottons were hospitality itself.

Jean had turned out to be a vivacious redhead, as bubbly as her shock of short red curls suggested, and Vinny knew that they would hit it off at once. She was a little younger than Vinny and was at teacher training college back in England most of the year, spending the long vacations with her parents in Spain. She had lived on and off in Granada for the last four years and spoke a fluent and extrovert dialect which seemed to Vinny to imply a familiarity with circles somewhat less respectable than those in which her parents moved. But she had her mother's sweetness of temperament and seemed ready to fling herself entirely into the role of tour guide during Vinny's few days' respite before work started in earnest.

'You must come up to the Alhambra today,' she cried, bounding into Vinny's room unannounced on the third morning. She still had on her short white cotton nightdress, its ribbons trailing haphazardly as she burst in through the door.

'Honestly, Vin, it's amazing! I never cease to be astounded by it. Of course,' she added with a grin, 'it's at its best with a lover or two by one's side, but despite that, I don't see why we can't enjoy it *a dos*!'

Vinny was rueful. 'I feel really groggy still. It's my shoulder, I suppose. And the heat. I seem to be taking time to adjust to being here. I'm not usually as languid as this!' She yawned and lay back among the pillows.

Jean looked sympathetic. 'It is horribly muggy just now,' she agreed. 'Just your bad luck to arrive at a time like this. But it won't be like this for long, you can count on that.' She sighed. 'I'm just no good in the sun, worse luck. You should be O.K., though, with plenty of suntan lotion. With your blonde hair I bet you'll look fantastic with a tan. Personally I prefer winter here. I know it's heresy to say a thing like that! But it's such a lively place anyway, with all the foreign students, and the Alhambra isn't overrun by tourists then either.'

She bounced down on to Vinny's bed. 'I'm at a

bit of a loose end, actually. I thought Denny was coming over. It was a hell of a blow to hear he'd broken his leg and wouldn't be coming.'

Denny was the friend of the friend who had helped arrange Vinny's accommodation.

'I'm no substitute, I'm afraid,' said Vinny.

'Hell, I didn't mean that, but you know. . . .' Jean grimaced.

Vinny told her that Denny asked to be remembered.

'Stiff upper-lip Englishman. The darling! I'm mad about him—I think! And I suspect he's mad about me too.' She smiled complacently. 'I suppose I shouldn't say that, it's tempting fate, but I don't care. Mum and Dad are very much against him at the moment, but I'm hoping if we play it cool they'll come round to my way of thinking.'

'I can't imagine you'd want your father to be mad about him!' remarked Vinny with a grin.

Jean laughed. 'Just a little less silent disapproval would suit me. Just because he's got no money. Oh hell, they're not snobs, not really, but they do go on a bit. They call it being practical. But I won't start in on all that now. You know what parents are like.'

'Mm,' replied Vinny noncommittally. What Jean was saying was at the moment too close to home. 'Actually I think sometimes they can be right.'

She swung down quickly off the bed to forestall further questions. The thought had struck her that she was still working out her feelings about Zak torn between anger, relief, hurt pride and regret, at how unsatisfactory things had been between them.

She had thought she was in love, but maybe it

had been something else after all. But in that case how could she trust her own feelings? Had it just been the ease of companionship that had appealed to her? Sharing something, paintings, music, discovering new ways of looking at things?

Zak had been like a brother to her. Certainly she didn't feel any sense of loss now—just this vague heaviness and lack of energy, and an uncertainty which seemed to be based on anger at herself for dreaming away so much of the summer and being taken in, if her parents' suspicions were well founded, by his self-seeking attitude. On that score she had decided to reserve judgment until they met again.

'You look thoughtful,' probed Jean. 'Someone back home?'

'Not really,' replied Vinny with a bemused look. 'Sometimes, you know, I think we can imagine we're in love—but we're in love with love, not with the person. Know what I mean?'

Jean shrugged. 'This is the place to be in love with love. You've chosen it all right. Wait until your hear the nightingales on the Hill of the Alhambra!' She jumped up. 'Come on, we'll leave the sightseeing till later if you're not feeling very energetic. Today I'll show you the student quarter and then we'll have a drink in El Suizo. Enough of all this mooning about.'

Vinny yawned. 'I know you're right. I'll be at work soon, then you'll have no chance to show me around. I really must make an effort!'

'To make it easier,' grinned Jean, 'come and have breakfast on my balcony. Luisa's making chocolate right now. After that, we'll go straight into town.'

'How are you feeling really?' asked Jean, when, refreshed and wearing a cool print dress and strappy sandals, Vinny finally emerged to greet the day.

'My shoulder's still a little stiff, but otherwise I'm all right.' She yawned, and both girls burst out laughing. 'Oh dear,' apologised Vinny. 'I just don't know why I'm so tired. I feel so exhausted.'

'We'll take it easy today, then. Just a little café-ing, perhaps?'

'I think I can cope with that,' grinned Vinny.

'You don't mind missing out on the Alhambra?'

'It's not as if I've only got a few days' holiday to spare. I'd rather wait until the weather's right so I can see it at it's best.'

'You think I'm overrating it, don't you?' said Jean as she poured the traditional Spanish break-fast drink of thick sweet chocolate. 'You'll see. You've a real treat in store. Now tell me about this man at the station.'

'Which man?' asked Vinny lifting her head.

'The hero of the moment. The one who saved your life. Did you manage enough Spanish to thank him?'

'I managed,' replied Vinny, blushing at the memory of her outburst. 'He seemed to speak ex-cellent English anyway. I don't think he felt in the need for thanks. He was just doing what a man like him would have to do.'

She stirred her cocoa, watching the blob of fresh cream dissolve round the edges.

Jean looked up sharply. 'You sound a bit disen-chanted,' she remarked.

'Well, he was jolly arrogant,' burst out Vinny.

'You should have seen the way he looked at me afterwards in the station buffet—as if I was something the cat brought in!'

'Oh,' smiled Jean, knowing, 'one of the *señoritos* eh!'

'One of the what?' demanded Vinny.

'*Señoritos,*' repeated Jean, lolling back on the wicker chair and grinning knowingly at her. 'There's a certain type of man over here who cultivates a kind of superior elegance of manner which seems to entail a complete disdain of everyone and everything, especially women—unless,' she added, 'they're of a certain type themselves—you know, hair scraped back, cheekbones you could sharpen a knife on, full of hauteur—and in my opinion utterly boring. The one deserves the other, actually.'

'I don't understand,' said Vinny, looking perplexed. 'He was certainly pretty sure of himself. I mean, I felt he was really looking down his nose at me at first. He thought I was a tourist travelling on the cheap just because I came by train.' She paused. 'I suppose I did look a bit of a mess, but even so. . . .'

'You'll meet plenty of his type in certain circles. Mostly the sort of men Dad seems to know, as it happens—bankers, agriculturalists, canning factory owners and the like. It's all a sort of affectation. Though often they don't even have wealth to back up their arrogance—all style and no substance. But they all have one thing in common: *pundonor.*'

'What's that?' asked Vinny.

'It's an overblown sense of honour, pride. They

cultivate it. It makes them very cool, very aloof, very proud. Their women wear flounced flamenco dresses and ride side-saddle behind the men on expensive thoroughbreds at the Seville Fair.'

'Sounds picturesque, but not like real life. More like something out of a travel brochure.'

'Oh, it is, it is,' said Jean. 'But don't take any notice of me. I'm just full of sour grapes. I mean, my poor darling Denny doesn't stand a chance in that scene, does he? He's not tall enough for a start.' She laughed ruefully. 'Secretly I think Mum hoped I'd set out to catch a specimen like that. But can you see me riding side-saddle behind any man? No fear!' She flicked a piece of croissant over the edge of the balcony and a couple of waiting sparrows scrambled for it from out of the bushes shading the lawn. 'Still, enough of that. I don't expect you'll be seeing *him* again. At least you can thank your stars he was so quick off the mark.'

Lavinia shuddered at what would have happened if her rescuer had been a second or two later. 'He said I should light a candle to someone,' she told Jean.

'Good idea,' replied Jean somewhat unexpectedly. 'I always believe in following local customs. We'll find an appropriate church for you when we're down town. Best to keep on the right side of fate as far as you can.' She rose to her feet. 'Feel ready to start now?' she asked.

Vinny finished the remains of her chocolate. 'All ready,' she smiled.

Jean ushered her to the door. 'We'll have a nice quiet introduction to Granadine café society,' she promised. 'Nothing too strenuous. I feel like having a nice lazy day too.'

It was nearly midday by the time they got into town. Jean had a little English sports car and the two girls left it in the Plaza Neuva, which was as near to the centre of the town as they could get without getting snarled up in the midday traffic jams. She handed the keys to an attendant and, catching Vinny's look of surprise, said airily, 'Oh, it's O.K. I'm blocking that Mercedes. José will move me if the driver wants to get out before we come back. I tip him well and he does the rest. It's a neat system. Nothing bureaucratic like parking tickets and meter maids to worry about.'

The one-legged attendant was already taking some keys from another driver.

'Come on, let's meet the midday crowd at El Suizo's,' said Jean.

It was a short walk along the crowded boulevard to the main square. Vinny looked round for a sign to show where they were going, but there was only one large café on the opposite side of the road. It had large plate glass windows, rather grand revolving doors, and an ice-cream parlour, all chrome and plate glass, to one side.

Automatically she read the name above it and a sudden shiver went through her. 'El Gran Café', it said in chrome lettering.

'Come on,' said Jean, pulling her across the road.

'But is that where we're going?' Vinny pulled back.

'That's right,' replied Jean. 'That's El Suizo's.'

'But that's not what it says,' demurred Vinny.

'No. But the locals all know it as El Suizo's on

account of some Swiss bloke who used to run it years and years ago. The name stuck. And it's been famous ever since as a hang-out for all the poets and musicians and toreros who pass through this way. Honestly, Vinny, don't be put off by the way it looks. It's not an old ladies' tea-room, even though it's a real period piece,' Jean rattled on in full flight. Vinny could only dodge along behind her as they risked life and limb to cross the busy road. Her eyes were darting from side to side— but it wasn't traffic she was on the look-out for.

Jean was saying, 'Probably even the waiters are the same. Wait till you see inside. It just goes to show what Granada used to be like in the mad days before the civil war—when every second man you'd meet would be a revolutionary poet or a doomed and beautiful matador, or at least, one of the *cantaors* who immortalised them. That's how the books tell it, and there are plenty of books written about the place. Even now everybody seems to be a flamenco singer or a film star——'

They had reached the revolving doors and Jean was still talking. She flung out her arms, oblivious to the stares of the passersby.

'You are now about to set foot within the famous portals of myth and magic——'

But before they could go on, somebody was already coming through the doors, briskly pushing them round so that they revolved with dangerous rapidity. Jean plunged in and Vinny was just about to follow suit when the person already inside was whirled out on to the pavement, almost colliding with her as she waited to slot herself into a vacant space. It was a man, and he stopped in mid-stride when he saw her.

Vinny gaped.

He seemed to incline his head with an almost imperceptible movement. His face, with its expression of hauteur, was otherwise blank as his dark, brooding eyes raked her body.

The doors went on revolving uselessly with no one in them. Vinny had a fleeting impression of Jean's face peering out at her from the other side as if to find out why she hadn't followed through.

The man, after allowing his glance to travel over her, moved his lips in greeting. 'Buenos,' he said curtly, and before she could bring the unpractised greeting to her lips, he had resumed his rapid pace down the street and was soon lost in the crowd.

With a shudder Vinny slipped quickly into the next space and was revolved slowly inside the decelerating doors to find herself being thrust inside the café.

Once in, she stopped. She scarcely took in the size of it. Marble floors and stuccoed ceilings, with panelling of deep, polished mahogany around the little booths which lined the walls, the place was confusing in the animation of its clientele and the ceaseless movement of its ageing waiters.

It was true what Jean had said. There was a distinct feeling of having stepped back in time to the pre-war years, when a rather untidy elegance was in vogue. Even the waiters matched the grandeur of the decor, for they all wore black tail-coats and carried white napkins carelessly over their arms, like waiters in some old-style black and white movie.

But it wasn't this which now made Vinny stand,

her body by turns hot and cold, her thoughts in wild confusion.

'You look as if you've seen a ghost,' laughed Jean. 'I know it's a shock, this place, but are you O.K.?'

'It's not that. It's—something else. . . .' Vinny bit her lip. What could she say? There was nothing to explain.

'Come on, tell me in a minute. Let's find a table in the middle where we can be seen.'

Jean plunged off through the forest of tables to an empty one which gave a good view over the rest of the café but also managed to be a focal point for the eyes of the other customers. Rapidly a waiter approached, obviously pleased to see one of his regular customers, and Jean ordered two *cafe solos* and something from the cake stand.

'Well, have you recovered?' she asked when they were comfortably seated.

'It was that man,' said Vinny quietly at last. 'It was such a shock seeing him like that—nearly bowling me over again.'

'Which man?' demanded Jean.

'The one coming through the doors as we came in. He was the one I told you about at the station the day I arrived.'

The Cottons had insisted that Vinny tell them everything that had befallen her that day, and she had told them—well, almost everything.

Jean grinned. 'That one? How extraordinary! The Hero? The Man Who Saved Your Life?'

Vinny smiled despite herself. 'All right, goon, I'm not trying to make anything out of it. It's just——' she wrinkled her nose, 'he makes me feel sort of scared somehow, and horribly confused.' And, indeed, her hands were shaking.

Jean shrugged. 'Maybe there's a good reason. Did he speak to you?'

'He just said, *"Buenos"* and walked off.' Vinny blushed slightly. She hadn't explained the bit about the lunch date. Jean would no doubt think it was a hoot, being picked up like that before she'd even set foot outside the station. But the man himself had obviously not been pleased at having been stood up—though that wasn't what had happened at all, thought Vinny ruefully. With a regretful little sigh she realised that she would have gone to meet him if only she hadn't overslept that first day.

Jean gave a glance towards the revolving doors. 'I can't say whether or not he's one of the crowd I know,' she told Vinny, 'I didn't get a chance to have a proper look at him. But we're sure to see him again, especially as he's an habitué of this place. It does rather suggest, though, that he's one of those impoverished *señoritos*—all style and no pesetas. You don't get the better sort coming here, hob-nobbing with the bohemian riff-raff.'

'What about us?' queried Vinny with a little pout.

Jean shrugged this aside with a grin.

'Anyway,' Vinny went on, 'he certainly seemed all right. Like somebody used to giving orders. That sort of authority often goes with the right background.' It seemed important to defend him against Jean's criticisms.

But her friend merely shrugged. 'In the country of *pundonor* who can tell?' she told her. 'Don't be taken in by the gigolo type. They always play up the high style. It attracts a better class of woman.'

'Jean!' Vinny was truly shocked. 'I'm sure he's not——' Then she stopped, and her eyes clouded. Here she was already making excuses for a man she'd met only once, just as she used to make excuses for Zak when her parents criticised him. She tried to pull herself together. 'You're probably right,' she said lamely.

'This isn't England,' Jean laughed airily. 'There are different rules here. A good-looking man can make quite a nice living, thank you very much, if he plays his cards right. There are plenty of rich foreign widows around who are willing to pay for their comforts.'

Vinny didn't say anything.

'You look shocked,' said the younger girl. She started to giggle. 'Aren't I awful? He's probably a very respectable married man just going about his daily business, like rescuing young Englishwomen from death, and having cups of coffee down town.' She was still giggling when the waiter arrived with their gateaux on a silver salver and two tiny cups of thick black coffee.

'*Gracias,*' said Jean amiably, and the waiter bowed his head with a gesture that would have been deferential if there hadn't been some trace of an inner pride which seemed to suggest connections with a noble past. But Vinny scarcely noticed this. For some reason Jean's words had set a momentary cloud over her and she gazed at the ever-revolving doors for some time without being able to find anything to say.

Fortunately they were soon joined by a succession of Jean's friends and the redheaded girl began to hold court. She was obviously popular and she was in such a good humour, rapidly exchanging jokes and snippets of gossip with the people who stopped off at their table, that Vinny was happy to allow herself to drift with the mood of the moment. Jean tried to keep up a constant translation from Spanish for Vinny's benefit, but several of her friends were young Americans and her Spanish friends were eager to practise their English too. Despite all this going on around her, Vinny felt her glance steal towards the revolving doors more than once, and it was during one of these momentary lapses into the privacy of her own jumbled thoughts that she realised Jean had been trying to attract her attention.

'I'm sorry,' she said in confusion. 'My head's simply reeling with so much Spanish. It's more than I can take in all at once.'

Jean smiled. 'I was just saying we'll do the shops in a bit, then pop back home for siesta. We can freshen up, then meet Ricky, Paco and Co. down town for a bite to eat before we go there.'

'Sorry,' said Vinny, not following, 'go where?'

'To Curro's.'

Vinny looked blank.

'Didn't you follow that?' Ricky broke in. 'I was telling Jean about a new *cantaor* who's at Curro's tonight. That's a flamenco club, the best in town. We heard this new singer last night, and he's amazing. We just happened to drop in thinking it was going to be the usual visitors' night, but it was electric. He's some unknown, but believe me, he's going to be a name. They've booked him for one more night.'

'We'd better eat fairly early,' said Jean. 'You know what it's like when there's anyone new on the scene. Word spreads like wildfire and the place will no doubt be packed out. Do you fancy that, then?' she asked, turning to Vinny.

'Sounds terrific,' nodded Vinny. 'I was hoping to hear some authentic flamenco—I'm interested in singing myself. Of course,' she added hastily, 'only very English stuff, Elizabethan court songs mainly——'

'At opposite poles of the musical spectrum, I should say,' observed Ricky. 'It should be interesting to compare the two.' He looked owlishly over his glasses at her, but she wasn't in the mood to start a serious conversation about music. 'We'll see you about ten,' he resumed, turning back to Jean.

'That's a date. But what about a meal first?'

'I've got lessons this evening and I'm not sure I'll be able to get away in time.'

'If you do, well and good,' said Jean easily, 'otherwise see you at the Club.' She turned to Vinny when the group moved off. 'They're a fun crowd,' she said. 'Let's mosey down town now and see what else is going on.'

They spent the rest of the day wandering round the shops, then, as everything began to close down for the afternoon rest period, the two girls wended their way back to the car.

The one-legged attendant had indeed moved Jean's Triumph in order to let out the Mercedes, and Vinny idly speculated on how he had managed to drive either car with such a disability.

The sky was still overcast and the air damp and heavy, was like a steam bath, even though they drove along with the roof back. 'We'll have a drive on to the Vega some time,' said Jean as she changed into bottom gear to climb the steep drive to the villa. 'It's quite unlike anywhere back home. The villages are like something out of one of those tell-it-like-it-is, this is the authentic West, cowboy movies. Lots of tall dark men lounging around inside dimly lit bars as the noonday sun brings passions to the boil. There's always a lot of smouldering eye-talk going on. Blood feuds go back generations—duels to preserve the family honour and so on, all simmering beneath a surface of ultra-cool respectability. Outwardly everything is calm and rather formal.'

Vinny climbed languidly out of the car. She felt pleasantly tired by the day's activities. But she turned back to Jean with a teasing smile. 'Are you making all this up?' she teased. 'Everybody I've met so far seems quite ordinary, no different from most of the folks back home. I'm beginning to suspect that this picture of the exotic Andalusian temperament is just a myth. I mean——' she went on, teasingly, as they walked slowly across the patio, 'look at all those respectable-looking people in El Suizo's taking morning coffee. I was quite disappointed. I can't imagine any of them being involved in blood feuds or duels in the sun.'

'Don't you believe it,' promised Jean. 'Be prepared—there'll be fireworks tonight all right, even if it is just the music.'

Vinny soon retired to her room after a light lunch on the patio with Jean and her mother. She still felt strangely enervated and it seemed to be too much trouble to put her mind to anything at all. Her Spanish phrase book lay unopened beside her damaged leather bag, and she looked guiltily at it before flopping languidly down on the bed. She had meant to replace the leather bag when she went round the shops with Jean, leatherware was cheap and of first class quality here, but she had been unable to make a simple choice between the designs on display. 'Oh, come on,' she had said to Jean after standing perplexed before an array of shoulder bags in their third shop. 'Let's admit it, I'm just not in a spending mood today. It's no good trying to buy anything in this state. I'll only regret it tomorrow.'

Now she sighed and let her eyes close. She had a fleeting picture of a curly-haired boy smiling dreamily into the distance before sleep came down suddenly to claim her.

'Wakey-wakey!' Tousled red hair bobbed into her range of vision as her eyes slowly opened. For a moment she didn't know where she was—there was a throbbing pain in her shoulder and a man's voice was saying, 'Better your papers scattered in disarray than yourself.' Then she was fully awake, and stretching like a cat. A yawn overtook her, then another and another, and Jean laughed.

'It's six o'clock already. When I saw how sound asleep you were earlier I thought I maybe ought to let you sleep on.'

Vinny made a show of scrambling energetically out of the bed, but it was an energy she did not feel. 'I'm sorry I feel so dopey—I don't know what's wrong with me. Give me a minute to come

to.' She stood up, yawning again. 'It must be the
change of climate. I've also had a very lazy summer
so far. That seems to make one tired, don't you
think?' She caught sight of herself in the mirror on
the dressing-table and paused critically. 'I do look
washed out, don't I? I don't think I'm always as
pale as this.'

'It's nothing that a little bit of sunshine won't
put right,' said Jean helpfully. 'This cloud won't
last forever.' She looked at her watch. 'Can you be
ready in an hour?'

'Of course,' Vinny replied. 'I'll have a quick
shower to get me going again.' She stretched languidly once more and gave Jean a reassuring smile.

Later that evening they were making their way
to the Club after a pleasant little meal in a down-
town *comedor*. Ricky and Co had left a message
to say that they were all coming on later. 'It's
mainly a question of money,' explained Jean.
'They're all students and though their families are
mostly comfortably off they go through periodic
bouts of financial restraint. As it's near the end of
term I expect this is one of them.' They chatted
amicably as they walked through the busy streets
to the club. The city seemed to be alive with activity, although it was nearly ten o'clock.

'I'll say one thing,' grinned Vinny, 'the old place
back home wouldn't be throbbing with life at this
time of night.' She had a momentary picture of the
place where she had grown up with its very English
village green, its grey Saxon church, half-timbered
inn and glass-fronted supermarket ranged for all
the world like something from a film set. All outward activity ceased at five-thirty sharp when the

shops closed during the week, and there wasn't even a youth club disco to bring a little life into the long evenings. A cricket match, perhaps, would go on in the nearby stray for as long as the light lasted, but it was all a far cry from the glittering ceaseless to-ing and fro-ing of people on the wide boulevards around the Plaza de Bib-Rambla.

Jean turned off down a dimly lit alley and they followed the crowd till they came to a small neon sign above a heavy timbered door. 'This is it. Let's hope we can find a seat near the stage,' said Jean, as they threaded their way through the people round the Bar to the stairs which led down into the basement. 'I don't expect the gang to be here just yet, so it's as well to be early to get a seat.'

She was right about the gang. They were no-where in evidence, but the girls found a suitable table next to the little raised stage in the tiny base-ment room, and spread their things out in the hope of being able to save a few seats for when the others arrived. One or two people stood around the bar at the far end, and many of the tables were already taken up. A waiter came over straight away, and Jean ordered a bottle of *tinto*.

'Denny and I used to come here a lot,' explained Jean, giving a rueful glance at a couple who were sitting with linked fingers across the candlelit table next to their own. 'I always think of Granada as a city for lovers. It's far more romantic and less hackneyed than Paris.' She gave a sidelong look at Vinny. 'I hope you meant what you said earlier about having no-one back home. This isn't the place to be if you want an easy time with any promises to be faithful and true. Far too many temptations!

'I've had enough of moonlight and roses,' said Vinny quickly. 'I'm travelling solo for a while.'

'Tell me about him,' asked Jean shrewdly.

'There's nothing to tell,' answered Vinny truthfully. 'It was an affair that never got off the ground.' She shrugged. 'I think I know myself a little better now. And I'm looking forward to giving myself some space for a while. The last thing I intend is to get into a heavy romance with anyone here. I want to make a go of this job and get my future sorted out properly.'

Just then she looked up at some sort of commotion at the door. A crowd of five or six Spaniards, both men and women, had just come in. As they made their way towards the stage Vinny suppressed a gasp of surprise. One of the men, carrying a guitar, seemed very familiar. He turned, holding out his hand to help one of the women on to the stage. She was a tall, dark-haired beauty wearing huge gold gypsy ear-rings and a scarlet flamenco dress. As he turned his glance accidentally strayed to the table where Vinny and Jean were sitting. His eyes flickered over Vinny with no sign of recognition, and in a moment he had turned away and was busy setting up his guitar ready to play.

Vinny turned slowly to look at Jean. She gripped the edge of the table.

'That's him,' she breathed. 'That's the man from the station!'

CHAPTER FIVE

'HE's gorgeous! Why didn't you say so?' breathed Jean, her eyes devouring the tall figure of the man as he stood up to adjust one of the spotlights which were fixed to a corner of the brick arch which flanked one side of the stage.

Dressed from head to foot in black, the only other colour was the deep tan of the man's skin, and the light satiny grain of his guitar. His hair was almost blue-black, noted Vinny without emotion, blue-black like a figure from a travel poster. She didn't really believe people could have hair like that in real life. It was like some kind of dream. Jean was babbling on about *los señoritos*, her eyes, Vinny observed, never leaving the man's face.

'But don't you just hate that type, though?' she was saying now. 'I hate men when they're too good-looking. They're always so arrogant. This one looks like a particularly conceited specimen. He probably hasn't got two halfpennies to scratch together, but because he's got looks and a guitar he thinks he owns everything.' Her eyes were calculating. She turned to Vinny. 'He can't be all that good either, otherwise we'd know who he was. At his age flamenco singers are already well known if they're any good at all.'

'How old do you think he is?' asked Vinny.

Jean looked back at the man and shrugged. Then she poured them both another glass of *tinto* almost without noticing what she was doing. 'Dad wants me to marry a banker,' she said unexpectedly. 'Can you imagine anything more deadly boring? I don't know why suitors have to have pots of money before they're acceptable to one's parents.'

Vinny didn't answer. She was gazing with a kind of leaden feeling at the two women in the group. One of them was in her thirties, a glorious buxom woman with a dress so tight Vinny wondered how she could breathe. It clung like a second skin to her voluptuous body, but at mid-thigh the scarlet satin material seemed to explode in a burst of frills which flashed provocatively to reveal olive tanned legs every time the woman turned. Her expression was full of hauteur, but when she smiled or made some rapid comment over a provocatively raised brown shoulder to the men in the group, there was all the allure of a mature woman's charm in its promise. She was saying something now in a rich sultry accent to the man with the guitar, and the smile which had dazzled Vinny already that time in the station buffet illuminated the sombre levels of his face with breathtaking suddenness.

The basement had miraculously filled up as if a crowd had been waiting for just this appearance and the spare seats at the table which Jean had hoped to save had been snapped up in the crush. People pressed in on all sides and Vinny had to crane her neck to see the other performers. There were two other men, one of whom was evidently some sort of manager or compère, as he was busy now rearranging the straight-backed wooden chairs in a formal line across the stage while the other one, in his early fifties, wearing a casual open-necked shirt and check trousers with high-heeled leather boots, was sitting with his hands resting lightly on his knees in a position of surprising calm in view of the excitement the group was creating. Neither had the dark arrogance of Vinny's rescuer, and indeed the manager, though of similar age, late twenties or early thirties, was affably fielding the goodnatured badinage which was being thrown at him by a group of people at a nearby table, in a manner which bespoke a more easygoing and amiable nature than promised by the guitarist's saturnine expression.

The other female member of the group, Vinny noted dully, was as alluring as the woman he had helped up on to the stage, but as an almost polar opposite to her colleague. Whereas the other woman was voluptuously mature in manner and appearance, the other one was slim, almost skinny, with a fragile, almost doll-like beauty that made her look not much more than fourteen or fifteen. The older woman had her dark hair coiled in a sophisticated arrangement of loops and kiss-curls, embellished with one dramatic blood-red carnation. The young girl on the other hand had left her waist-length black hair loose and wore a single white clematis flower nestling demurely in its sleek fronds. Her eyes were modestly downcast most of the time, but when she now and then shyly raised them they were large and dark and full of a beguiling innocence.

Vinny observed the group without emotion before turning to Jean. 'I wonder how a man chooses between those two,' she said wryly. 'It's not fair. They both look so dramatically appealing yet in such different ways.' She glanced down at her own pale skin and twirled a strand of her ash-blonde hair between two fingers. 'I feel so insipid by comparison.' She yawned languidly too as if unconsciously emphasising her lack of drama. She sighed. Even Jean looked vibrantly alive, despite the competition. She was wearing a black dress which plunged to a deep V, showing off her cleavage with its milky white skin to advantage. Her hair was prettily tousled and her green eyes flashed mischievously as she caught the eye of the compère. He stopped for an instant to throw her a smile and his lips parted in some exclamation which Vinny was about to consign to her long list of Spanish words as yet unlearned. With an effort she roused herself. 'What did he say?' she asked.

'Guapa,' said Jean, with a self-satisfied smile. 'Beauty, smashing. He's rather sweet himself, isn't he?'

Vinny grimaced. 'That's more than you can say about that one.' She nodded towards the guitarist and managed to suppress an unaccountable shiver which ran through her. There was a dangerous and unpredictable air about the guitarist which she did not wish to explore.

'He'd be more than I could handle, the younger girl admitted grudgingly. 'I'm quite content to sit here and just look at him, the gorgeous beast.' Whatever she said next was drowned in the sudden applause which broke out from all around them as the compère came forward with his hand upraised. He welcomed everyone to the evening's performance in a rapid Spanish dialect which even Jean said she found difficult to follow. As far as Vinny

could guess he introduced the evening's enter-
tainers, though. The rest of the group seemed to be
well known to the audience. Jean explained in a
low voice that the *aficionados* of this type of music
were great critics of the relative merits and talent
of the performers. New or otherwise unknown solo
performers would sit in with the local group,
usually travelling from club to club in order to
make a living and to establish a name for themselves, and these soloists would be dancers, or singers—*cantaors*, that is—or guitarists. The previous
night the unknown guitarist had met with such
success that he had been invited back for the rest
of the week. And the management of the club
would already be congratulating themselves on
their find as confirmed by tonight's turn-out.

'Where's he been hiding himself?' murmured
Jean in the lull before they started. 'If he's as good
as they're claiming, he must be known somewhere
else.' She gave a sceptical little smile. And then the
music started.

It was, as Ricky had told them in El Suizo's,
electric.

The two women and the leader were well loved
and respected and met with thorough approval tonight from an audience who knew them well. But the
guitarist was an unknown quantity with rumours
of an already high standard of playing to live up to.

But after a few minutes' opening there was no
doubt in the minds of those who knew what they
were talking about. Here was a magical performer
of an exacting art. The man played like an angel
possessed—sensitively echoing the nuances of the
singers' every intonation, drawing them on with the

skill and precision of the matador, supporting the dancers in the intricacy of their stylised movements, then driving them all on with the rich full-bodied sound of a guitar played at full stretch to a climax. One minute he was caressing the strings like the most sensitive of lovers, the next playing hard driving chords with a whiplash precision which sent the audience into a frenzy of adoration.

Lavinia found herself leaning forward with both elbows on the table, her lips lightly parted, scarcely breathing with suspense as she followed the intricate musical pyrotechnics of the man's playing. When a particularly daring sequence was executed with faultless precision she sat back, brushing a stray lock of pale hair from her brow, her breath released in one sigh of satisfaction.

Here was a fire and a daring she had never before suspected. It was as if she had come alive for the first time. Her body felt charged with energy as vibrantly as if plugged directly into some mystical energy source.

When the shouting and cries of 'Olé!' had died down and there was a momentary respite as the singer left his seat and came to stand at the front of the stage, Jean leaned across to Vinny.

'I take back what I said earlier,' she whispered. 'The man's magic. The Spanish word is *duende*, the dark angel.' She sat back and let her eyes drink in the scene before her. 'I guess he has it.'

The rest of the evening seemed to pass in a blur for Lavinia. The performance itself was less than an hour, but given the intensity and sheer creative invention of the performers an hour was a long time.

When they all got up to leave the stage, she felt drained with a totally unexpected sense of exhaustion, as if some deep part of her soul had been tapped for the first time. All round them the audience was sitting tight, roaring its approval, refusing to budge until the performers came back to give them some more of their potent magic. The manager of the club appeared, emphatic in his assurance that that was the end for the time being.

'There's Ricky and Co.,' said Jean suddenly. She waved, but just as Ricky saw them, he and the rest of the gang were swept out in the sudden exodus by an audience who had no intention of sitting around all night looking at an empty stage.

'Let's go,' said Jean, getting up abruptly. 'Come on, before we lose them in the crush.' In a trice she had slipped into the crowd and was being borne along towards the exit. Vinny paused for a moment, without the energy to tear herself away from the place, but when she saw Jean already halfway up the steps to street level she roused herself enough to stand up and let the crowd carry her with it.

There was quite a jam in the doorway and it was a few minutes before she found herself being disgorged along with the mob on to the street. She looked round, expecting to see Jean and the rest of the group, but there were so many people standing around in animated groups in the little alleyway that she could see no sign of the now familiar faces. Unperturbed, she let the crowd take her with it to the end of the road, but when she came to the wide boulevard at the junction she was dismayed to find that there was still no sign of her redhaired friend.

She turned back towards the club, finding it difficult this time to walk against the flow of people, but she steadily made her way forward despite the easily understood invitations of a number of men in which the new-learned word *'guapa'* figured. Blushing at finding herself, because unaccompanied, the focus of their attentions, she tried to walk a little quicker as if with some urgent destination in mind. But when she reached the club there was nothing to do but stand around and wait. Already the upstairs bar was empty and there were only one or two men hanging around, a little the worse for *tinto*, she guessed, eyeing them out of the corners of her eyes.

One of them detached himself from his comrades and came over to her. She hadn't a clue what he was saying; but guessed his meaning pretty quickly.

He came lurching forward towards her, so she turned and tried to move off. The man, however, had other ideas and shambled after her with a laugh. She quickened her pace, too late realising that she was now walking away from the main thoroughfare and that the alley was at its opposite end in gloomy shadow where the tenements rose up on either side of the cobbled passageway. The man was now right behind her and his two companions were leaning on the wall outside the club, watching their friend with evident amusement.

One of them seemed to shout some words of encouragement, for the man made a sudden grab, for an instant clutching Vinny tightly around the waist. As his hands moved up to fondle her breasts she gave him a sudden shove which momentarily sent him tottering back off balance against the wall.

It was enough to free herself. In an instant she was running off down the alley towards the dark. She ran to the bottom, then found to her dismay that it turned at a sharp right angle and continued on between tall unlit buildings which were all heavily shuttered. The man too had now reached the corner, and with a strange kind of drunken grunting sound seemed hellbent on pursuit. Vinny began to run fast now, blood pounding furiously in her temples. If she could only tell where the alley was leading she should know whether it could get her back to the main boulevard. From there surely she could shake off her pursuer in the well-lit and frequented centre of the town?

But the alley seemed to be winding back in the other direction and she had lost all sense of where she was. Mouth dry, she managed a quick look back over her shoulder and noticed with relief that she had already outstripped the drunk.

Breathless now, she slowed down to a brisk walk. As she approached the next corner she was already beginning to congratulate herself on a lucky escape when her blood froze in her veins.

There, lurching out of a gap between the tenements, was the drunk. A little out of breath, but definitely still in single-minded pursuit, he shambled towards her, completely blocking the way ahead. She let out a small scream and swung back in panic the way she had come. Another cry escaped her as she felt strong arms catch hold of her and the length of a man's body pressing against her own. She flung back her head and her thoughts churned in a turbulence of unexpected emotion.

The man who now held her in his arms was her rescuer from the previous day, the guitarist from Curro's.

Her look and exclamation of surprise brought a grim smile to his face. 'Don't you know better than to go walking unlit alleys in this part of town?' he asked her coldly. 'Women like you ask for trouble. Even I wouldn't want to wander around here too often alone.'

He held her away from him and his look of disdain was more than she could bear. She wriggled completely free from his arms and stood panting with the sudden release from fear, just a few paces in front of him. The drunk was forgotten. Her rescuer had said something to the man with an ill-concealed note of threat in his voice and the drunk had swiftly taken himself off, back into the shadows out of which he had come.

Now that she was free from immediate danger anger overcame her recent panic, forcing her to turn blazing eyes on the man.

'I didn't choose to walk down here alone. I'm not as stupid as you seem to think!'

'I suppose you were dragged down here,' he said. 'It matters not that I saw you with my own eyes calmly walking past the window of the club but a moment ago.'

'I was trying to escape from that man who was following me,' she replied icily.

'What a strange way to escape—to choose the narrowest and most ill-lit route in the quarter,' he answered cuttingly. 'A fine example of feminine logic, I must say.'

'That's not how it was!' exploded Vinny, clenching her fists with frustration. 'How was I supposed to know this was just a back street? You seem set on believing your own version of the truth. It seems there's no talking to you.' She turned angrily on her heel as if to set off in the opposite direction.

'Unless you intend to scale a twenty-foot wall you'll have difficulty in finding your way out that way,' the man smiled sardonically. 'I suggest you try talking with me. Perhaps I can show you a quick way on to the main boulevard, where no doubt your friends are waiting with some impatience for your arrival.'

She glared at him.

'Well,' he said easily, not moving, 'are you going to talk, or are all our conversations going to be conducted on the level of a full-scale argument?'

Vinny almost stamped her foot at the man's arrogance, but when he remained standing silently in front of her with no obvious intention of moving to let her either past or to show her the way back to the street, she had no alternative but to swallow her anger and speak in quieter tones. Even so, she found it a superhuman task to keep the ice out of her voice as she told him with exaggerated politeness that she would be most grateful if he would kindly guide her back to the road.

'Indeed I will,' he said with a slight formal bow, and taking her by the elbow he took her to the door of one of the shuttered buildings.

'Don't be alarmed,' he told her with a mocking glint in his eyes, 'this is the back of Curro's. My dressing-room, such as it is, overlooks the alley. That's how I saw you—through the shutters.' With

that he swung open the heavy oak door and Vinny
stepped through into a blaze of light.

It was an untidy room, with peeling stucco, and a
large ancient fan turning idly in the middle of the
yellowing ceiling. The other performers were
already on the point of leaving—the women now
wearing quite ordinary street clothes, the men un-
changed except for the cigars which they were pulling on with evident satisfaction. The older of the
two women came up to Vinny's rescuer and put
her arms round his neck. *'Caro,'* she murmured in
a throaty voice, and then there followed a stream
of what Vinny took to be Spanish endearments.
She could just make out something about the
woman being worried by his sudden disappearance,
but she said other things in a torrent of Spanish
with a flashing look in Vinny's direction which
spoke to her as eloquently as the most articulate
speech, and Vinny edged over to the far door, eager
to leave the man to his fiery companion. But he
was not letting her go so easily. With an abrupt
action he held the woman tightly for an instant,
then pushed her almost roughly to one side. Then
he was taking Vinny by the elbow once again and
ushering her through the door into the entrance
leading to the basement where he had performed
earlier.

'I'm quite all right now,' Vinny turned to him.
'It looks as if I have to thank you yet again for
helping me.'

'It seems that fate is playing some sort of trick
on us,' he said mockingly, 'and how your debts are
now piling up!'

'If there's anything I can do,' said Vinny guiltily,

'to show my gratitude. . . .' she tailed off. The meaning of the man's smile was unmistakable. 'Oh, this is impossible!' With a toss of her head she turned to the stairs leading up to street level.

'Not so fast.' The man pulled her back with a grip which was strong and firm but not rough. 'I think it would be advisable to call a taxi. The streets can be rather wild at this time of night, as you've discovered.'

'But as you said, my friends will be waiting for me somewhere outside——' she replied, not without a glimmer of satisfaction at being able to turn the man's words back on him.

'Then at least permit me to accompany you to the street.'

Brushing aside the protestations that rose at once to her lips, he walked her up the stairs into the now empty bar. The men who had been lounging around the doorway had gone and they walked in silence up the deserted alley towards the bright lights of the boulevard.

With a feeling of relief Vinny noticed a knot of people standing on the corner, among them the red hair of Jean was noticeable. She was talking animatedly to some people Vinny hadn't seen before. She turned to her companion. 'Thank you for escorting me to safety.' She said it with a hint of irony in her voice. 'I see my friends now. You needn't trouble to come any farther.'

'No trouble, no reward——' said the man with a mocking smile.

But before Vinny could cut in Jean turned at that moment and came rushing up to Vinny with an exclamation of relief. 'Well, I say, you're a dark

horse!' she cried when she recognised her escort.
'We thought we'd lost you.' She gave Vinny a sharp
look which spoke volumes. 'I see we needn't have
worried after all.' Clearly jumping to the wrong
conclusions, she was understandably piqued.
However, before Vinny could offer any explanation, Jean had turned vivaciously to the tall, dark
Spaniard with a radiant smile. 'I'd just like to thank
you for an incredible performance tonight,' she
said, looking into the man's eyes with no attempt
at concealing the light of hero-worship in them.
'That was a most astonishing evening.'

The man inclined his head. 'You're too kind,' he
replied in his impeccable English accent.

'We were all wondering why we've never heard
of you before,' went on Jean, focussing all her attention on the man.

'I have only just returned from several years in
South America,' he told her, eyeing the pretty redhead with a gleam of unmistakable approval in his
eyes.

'But you're not South American by birth?' asked
Jean, moving closer to him.

'No,' he paused and a half smile chased itself
across his face, 'despite my name.'

'Yes,' breathed Jean, 'El Brasiliano.' She paused
and her eyes never left the man's face. 'I think it's
a name we shall be hearing much of in the future.'

Again the man inclined his head in thanks, then,
ignoring Vinny, Jean began to talk to him in
Spanish so that he had to fall into step beside her
and together they walked slowly towards the boulevard.

Vinny had no option but to follow a pace or two

behind them. Jean seemed to be avidly plying the man with questions about his career, and evidently flattered, El Brasiliano stood for a further few minutes on the corner. Even if Vinny had wanted to join in she found they spoke too rapidly for her to make much sense of what they were saying. She stood on the edge of the group as everybody clustered round. It seemed to Vinny that they were making an unprecedented exhibition of themselves, talking exclusively to each other, apparently oblivious to their audience.

Vinny felt a tide of anger sweep over her. How ridiculous they all were to be fawning over the man like that! And how hypocritical Jean was to be so obviously smitten, after all she'd said earlier about *los señoritos*. As far as Vinny was concerned the man was as vain and unpredictable as he had first seemed, and she could find no good reason to change her mind just because he happened to be able to play and sing rather well. She waited huffily on the edge of the group, scarcely deigning to reply when Ricky eventually came over to ask her where she had got to earlier.

'I took a wrong turning,' said Vinny abruptly.

'Jean was quite worried,' he told her. 'We all were.'

'There was no need to be,' Vinny said sharply. 'I'm quite capable of looking after myself, you know.'

Ricky looked uncertain what to say for a moment, then he slowly drifted back to El Brasiliano's group of admirers. Vinny watched him go without remorse. How easily impressed they all were! They were just silly kids with no sense of dignity. The man was lapping up their childish praise as if it was something important. She watched Jean laugh vivaciously at something the man had said, then they were all suddenly moving off down the road.

The man turned to look at Vinny, but Jean at once claimed his attention and they moved off together in the middle of the group.

'Come on, Vinny,' called Ricky when he realised she wasn't following. 'We're going to Paco's.'

Vinny sighed. It would be bad manners to slope off now, even though she was tired out with a return of her earlier sleepiness which the performance had obviously only briefly dispelled. She decided to follow on, but even though they were walking slowly, she didn't try to catch up with them, but ambled on somewhere at the back, making a show of looking in shop windows whenever anyone tried to catch her eye.

No one had bothered to introduce themselves and the Spaniards, perhaps assuming she understood enough of the language, didn't bother to speak in English. Ricky had obviously taken her rebuff to heart and was now tagging along beside Jean, like the proverbial gooseberry.

Vinny wondered maliciously how the evening would turn out after all. Jean had promised fireworks, but somehow she couldn't see Ricky in the role of jealous lover, if, indeed, their relationship had gone so far. Now her eyes were opened to the ways of her hostess, thought Vinny darkly, she had no doubt the redhead had been consoling herself for the absent Denny with the ineffectual though handsome American.

What a bore, thought Vinny, trailing up to the door of the bar they had reached. I'll stick to the resolution I made before I came here: no more moonlight!

CHAPTER SIX

It was four in the morning by the time the party straggled out again into the Granadine dawn. The twin hills on which perched the Alhambra and the Generalife were tinged with rose and the two Moorish palaces looked as ethereal and full of romance as their legends claimed. But Vinny was unaware of this. All she could feel was a cold tiredness which made her wish she had followed her own first inclinations and left the group when they first decided to move on for one final drink.

Paco's had turned out to be a disco-bar with a small dance floor, and Jean had made it an opportunity to ensure that she never left El Brasiliano's side. By now, of course, everyone was on first name terms with him, and Carlos, though speaking little, had seemed content to remain at Jean's side, dancing with her in an abstractedly provocative way as if barely conscious of the effect his sinuous gyrations were having on the women and, in a different way, on the men, who formed a half admiring, half resentful audience around the pocket-sized dance floor.

The more Jean had seemed to throw herself at him, the more coldly distant from it all Vinny had felt, and when the dancing had continued, she had refused all invitations, so that by the end of the night she had been left in a little pocket of silence all by herself.

By herself, that was, except for Ricky. The American had soon realised that Jean's attentions were definitely fixed elsewhere and he too had become more and more morose as the night had progressed. He sat next to Vinny, the two of them lost in their own thoughts, separate, but united in their aloofness from the rest of the group.

It was with relief that the signs had been made for their imminent departure. With a wry smile Ricky helped Vinny on with her jacket. 'Not the most rewarding evening of our lives,' he said to her in an attempt to kindle some response even now.

'I'm sorry,' said Vinny, looking guiltily into his boyish face. 'I hope you don't think me very rude, I guess I'm just very tired.'

Ricky glanced jealously at Carlos and Jean. 'He certainly seems to have made a hit there. I thought she was more level-headed than that—making an exhibition of herself over a gigolo.' The look of disapproval on his face made him seem owlish again, for he had put his glasses back on, and for a moment Vinny felt sorry for the boy. It was as if she understood how jealousy over the loss of a loved one's affection could stab so piercingly into the soul, though of course that was nonsense, she chided herself. She was, fortunately, heart-free, and not herself prone to such sorrows.

Ricky put his arm lightly on her back to shepherd her towards the door after the others and when they got outside they saw that a couple of taxis had already been called. Ricky was on the point of making some tentative arrangement to meet Vinny down at El Suizo's the next day, though, she suspected, this was done more out of chivalry than for any other reason, as his attention was still in unguarded moments, on Jean and Carlos, when, to her surprise, she saw the girl getting into one of the taxis.

'Come on, Vinny,' Jean called, leaning out of the cab door to attract Vinny's attention. 'I'm too blotto to find the car. We'll go home by taxi.' Ricky seemed to give a cry of something like relief which he quickly stifled and he was almost smiling when Vinny turned to say goodnight. Carlos was standing by the taxi holding the door open and it was obvious, despite his attention to the niceties of chivalrous behaviour, that he wasn't coming with them.

Just before she stepped inside, he said quickly in English, 'I'm sorry if you were bored. I'm afraid Paco's was my idea.'

She looked blankly at him. 'Why should you be sorry?' she demanded. 'You seemed to be enjoying yourself.'

She climbed inside and sat down next to Jean, the door closed beyond her, and the taxi pulled smoothly away to the cries of *'Adios'* from the others, who were walking away in ones and twos or piling noisily into the second cab.

'I feel dreadful,' said Jean as soon as the taxi began to gather speed along the main road. 'I forgot to say goodbye to Ricky.'

'Yes,' said Vinny, pulling no punches, 'he was

quite cut up about tonight.' She wondered fleet-
ingly why she should feel so strongly. Ricky's jealousy was nothing to her, and what Jean did with
her men friends was her own affair. She tried to
soften her previous remark by saying lightly, 'Still,
you were rather monopolised by El Brasiliano. You
must be feeling pretty pleased with yourself.'

Jean looked at her sharply. 'To tell you the truth,
Vinny, I don't usually go overboard like this on
first meeting. The man's magic. I felt I was ignoring
everyone dreadfully, especially you. It was a bit
mean, when you don't really know anyone there. But
I just felt mesmerised by him. I couldn't help
myself.' She sighed. 'Not that he gave me much
encouragement, I'm afraid. I made all the running
there.'

'I didn't notice him making any strong objec-
tions,' teased Vinny trying to keep her voice from
shaking.

'No—well, I guess I'm quite a conquest from his
point of view—penniless street guitarist from some
obscure South American village being taken up by
foreign banker's daughter.' Jean laughed bitterly.
'I don't have many illusions about men, despite
my behaviour tonight.'

Vinny warmed to her friend's frankness. 'At least
you managed to lure him away from those two
dancers,' she said.

'For an evening, yes. But where do you think
he's going to wind up the rest of the night?' Jean
looked out of the window at the reddening dawn,
her face suddenly sober. 'Let's leave it. It was
a night out, that's all. I'm not so naïve that I'm
going to make a fool of myself over a man like that.'

Vinny gave a start of surprise. 'But you will see him again, surely?'

Jean turned clouded eyes to her companion. 'He didn't ask, actually. He merely drank what we offered, and danced with me because I asked him to, and he answered the questions everyone put to him with just enough information so as not to appear rude. But apart from that—nothing. He's hiding something, I'm sure of it.' She clenched her fists. 'Damn it! The man's totally unsuitable. Daddy would throw a fit if he thought I was getting involved with someone like that.'

Vinny's thoughts were in a strange turmoil after this. She felt mean at having harboured unkind thoughts about Jean all evening now that she knew the girl had not been enjoying things as much as she appeared, but she also felt dismayed to find that she was capable of feeling a slight shiver of satisfaction that El Brasiliano had not been as smitten by Jean as she had thought. Not that it's anything to me, one way or the other, she told herself angrily. Jean had said the man was unsuitable. He appeared to be an enigma. And he was obviously on the make. Of course, she argued with herself, if that were true, why had he not followed up his obvious opportunity with Jean?

'He'll be in touch,' she said emphatically, speaking aloud her private thoughts. 'Of course he will.'

Jean smiled, misunderstanding Vinny's reassurances.

'Do you really think so?' she sighed. 'Maybe you're right.' She gave a deep chuckle. 'I'd certainly make sure it was worth his while—without getting too involved, of course.'

She's irrepressible, thought Vinny, and was immediately down in the dumps again as she caught Jean's new-found confidence.

Next day Jean claimed to have an almighty hangover and jokingly begged to be excused further tour guide duties till her head returned to its usual consistency. 'It feels as if it's made up of millions of little bricks all jostling against each other,' she smiled wanly from the bed. 'How are you feeling?'

'Fine,' replied Vinny. 'Actually, quite fit.' She surprised even herself. She hadn't bothered to count the glasses of *tinto* which had seemed to appear as if by magic in front of her the previous evening. Jean gave her a hopeful look.

'I say, that's good news. You wouldn't be thinking of going into town at all, would you?' Vinny remembered her tentative date with Ricky, but as she had already made up her mind that she wouldn't encourage the boy she didn't think it worth mentioning.

'I'd half thought of trying to see the Alhambra after all,' she said. 'Despite the weather. At least it's not raining, and it seems a bit silly not to go up and have a look.'

Jean looked pleased. 'Then you probably wouldn't mind doing me a favour,' she said. 'I know you can drive.'

Vinny had told Jean on the evening they met that she had taken the precaution of getting an international driving licence just in case she wanted to hire a car in order to do a bit of sightseeing when time permitted.

'You wouldn't go and collect the car from

where I left it in the Plaza de los Lobos, would you?'

'Of course,' answered Vinny. 'No trouble. I can pick it up on my way back here.'

Jean threw the keys from her bedside table. 'You are an angel—thanks!'

Vinny had had to walk to the end of the lane in order to catch the bus which would take her to the Plaza Neuva. From there it was just a few minutes' walk up the narrow street which led eventually to the Alhambra. In all it took about an hour, and it was not yet ten-thirty when she found herself alighting in the square. She was already wishing she had worn something a little cooler than her cotton two-piece, for by the time the bus had trundled its way into town, the fabric was sticking unpleasantly to her body.

Undeterred, however, she set off up the Cuesta de Gomerez with its half-dozen or so one- and two-star hotels and its colourful shop fronts open to the street with their tourist wares invitingly displayed. She stopped to look at some long Spanish cloaks, romantically buckled and lined with different coloured satins. If things had been different, she thought, she might now be haggling with the shopkeepers over a price, intending to take one of the cloaks back home to someone. It was just the kind of impractical, beautiful garment Zak would enjoy wearing. If things had been different, that was what she would now be doing, she thought, overwhelmed by a sudden feeling of loneliness. But if things had been different, she scolded herself, she wouldn't be here now, alone, would she? With these not very profitable thoughts she dragged herself on up the hill.

It was a muggy day and she was beginning to regret setting out on the trip after all. She approached the outer entrance gates which straddled the road. Perhaps it would be best to go back into the town to pick up Jean's car and leave the sight-seeing till later? After all, the journey into town would not have been wasted, and perhaps she would even have a quick drink in El Suizo's after all. She was standing thus undecided on the pavement near the Puerta de las Grandas when she heard a voice quite close by saying in English, 'Good morning. Painting the town seems to agree with you.'

She looked up in surprise at being spoken to in this city of strangers and was astonished to find herself looking into the mocking eyes of El Brasiliano. She gulped, unable to think of an apt retort to his teasing remark. He seemed to look even more handsome in the full light of day, his hair gleaming brilliantly with a natural sheen that emphasised dramatically the deep tan of his skin. He was wearing the same black jacket, shirt and trousers as on the other occasions when she had met him and in the harsh light, with more leisure in which to take them in, she saw that Jean was right, he was just a penniless guitarist, for his clothes were threadbare at cuffs and collar. She couldn't imagine why she had thought him wealthy—at least, if his clothes were anything to go by he was certainly not. She assumed that it must have been the authoritative way with which he had pulled her to safety that had given her such a strong impression of command and authority. That, she thought wryly, and his high-handed attitude.

'Not bawling me out for once,' he remarked, after letting his eyes stray appraisingly over her body and come to rest at last on her face.

Vinny tightened her lips. 'So far,' she answered tartly, 'you haven't done anything to cause such a reaction.'

'So far,' he repeated with an amused chuckle. 'Better not count on it.'

'I wasn't going to.'

He paused. 'I've just had breakfast in my hotel, otherwise I would invite you for a cup of coffee.' He indicated one of the seedy *hosteles* farther down the hill. 'I believe you English take coffee about this time in the morning?'

'Sometimes,' she answered, 'but I'm on my way to see the Alhambra.' She had made up her mind all of a sudden. 'I'm being a tourist this morning,' she added, not without a little smile.

'That's better,' he said, softly, and unexpectedly. 'You look like an angel when you smile—so fair, so beautiful.'

Vinny felt herself blush and turned away, hating herself for being caught so unawares. Hell, she thought, here am I falling for a corny line like that from an obvious out-and-out philanderer!

It brought back an unwanted memory of Zak and an altogether different kind of caress in his voice, little like an angel. She turned stiffly, fighting to control her heart which was suddenly pounding wildly for no reason at all, but before she could say anything to cut him down to size, he had stepped on to the outside of the narrow pavement and was

already about to take her arm as if to accompany
her up the hill. She drew back.

'I would be pleased if you would do me the
honour of allowing me to accompany you. It has
been many years since I saw the old place and I can
think of no better way to spend the morning.'

Vinny felt caught. Without appearing rude there
was no excuse she could think of with which to
deflect him from his attention. 'It's an honour for
me to be accompanied by El Brasiliano,' she said,
matching the elaborateness of his speech and
adding a touch of irony of her own. With a small
smile he inclined his head and together they walked
slowly up the steep avenue in silence.

Vinny had expected him to assert his charm
without delay and was surprised that he didn't say
anything further until they came out near the
fountain just at the point where the avenue
snaked back on itself towards the massive Gate of
Justice.

'You were very quiet last night,' he observed.
'Don't you speak much Spanish?'

'Not a great deal. Not yet anyway.'

'I thought you told me you were working in
Granada?'

Vinny felt nettled. What was it to him what she
was doing here? She turned her best smile on him.
'Perhaps you were right,' she lied. 'Perhaps I am
just a tourist after all?'

He laughed aloud at this, his glance flickering
over the expensive shoes, the exclusive little suit,
and the gold chain she wore round her neck.
'You're obviously not travelling third class as you
seemed to be on the day you arrived.' He laughed

again, showing a flash of white even teeth, and Vinny became very conscious at the same time that she was dazzled by his looks, of the threadbare jacket, the cheap cloth, and the remarks Jean had made the night before.

Suddenly she felt very uncomfortable. Perhaps it was a mistake to let him think she was worth cultivating? At least he seemed to have forgotten that she hadn't turned up for their lunch date. Perhaps he now thought it was worth his while to swallow his pride?

She gave him a quick look which he was not too slow to intercept.

'So?' he breathed.

He seemed to move a step closer. She was acutely conscious of his height and the tough masculinity of his presence.

For a moment she thought he had misunderstood the look she had given him and was going to reach out to touch her. The hair prickled along the back of her neck and she took a small step back.

One or two people were sitting on the benches near the fountain, but even so the two of them seemed locked in a sudden intimacy which seemed to have an almost palpable force. It flashed between them like lightning and Vinny became hotly conscious of the feelings which he had aroused in her on her first day here, feelings which she had ever since been strenuously fighting to bottle up.

She felt a slow flush creep up the length of her body and the blood began to throb in her temples. She turned away, not sure whether he too had been aware of the sensation like an electric shock which seemed to shake through her.

The strange helplessness it brought in its wake made her voice hard as she told him abruptly that she wanted to get on and see the Palace without further delay.

Without waiting for his reply she set off briskly up the remaining few yards of the slope, and he was left to follow behind as she gained the shadowy entrance of the inner gate. It was a cobbled road which led again at right angles through the gloomy vault of the fortified keep, and Vinny pressed on, stumbling a little on the unevenness of the stones.

'*Atención!*' Coming up quickly beside her, he had put out a hand to steady her, and she sprang away as if his touch had indeed given her an electric shock.

'I'm not a cripple,' she said rudely, shaking off his hand.

'You're a very independent young woman,' he replied easily. 'Are we going to have our usual argument round about now?'

'I'm not interested in arguing for the sake of it,' she told him, 'merely in correcting any incorrect opinions about the nature of my own actions. I'm quite happy to walk along in silence. In fact, I'd prefer it.'

'My lady's wishes are my command,' he teased. 'If you'll allow me the odd word of Spanish approbation at the wonders soon to be displayed I promise to keep as silent as the tomb.'

' "As silent as the grave" sounds more idiomatic,' she told him coolly. 'Thank you for promising to be so compliant. I hope you can keep your promises.'

'I regard it as point of honour to keep promises,' he told her seriously.

'We shall see,' she smiled.

He was about to make some retort when he remembered what he had just said and quickly put his lips together, only the devilish spark in his eyes hinting at his evident mockery of her.

Vinny felt overcome by the handsomeness of his face, the brilliance of the smile which came and went so rapidly, illuminating the classic contours of his face. She had an overwhelming desire to feel his full, sensuous lips come down on hers, to surrender to the caress of skin on skin. With a sharp intake of breath she turned away, and, guidebook in hand, began the climb up the steps to the ticket office.

Carlos made no effort to pay for her entrance ticket but instead waited silently in the queue behind her as she used her few words of Spanish.

Then, all the way along the flower-lined path which led through the walled gardens at the foot of the Tower of Comares, she berated herself for her feelings which were being so easily aroused by such a man. Thoughts which seemed to have accentuated in her a twinge of loneliness not half an hour before seemed to have disappeared like chaff in the wind beside the devastating power of this new and more vibrant encounter. She felt as if she had never before known such a physical impact from a man's nearness as she did now with Carlos. At the same time she felt a kind of hollow despair in the pit of her stomach that he could never be anything to her, nor she to him.

Only by allowing herself to be duped into thinking his interest was without any ulterior motive
could she envisage surrendering herself to the
longing which he had aroused. She certainly didn't
intend to be caught twice in the same way. . . .

His silence now as they climbed the narrow steps
of the tower told her nothing of his feelings, nor
did the enigmatic expression on his handsome
face.

His thoughts could have been a million miles
away, and probably were, she thought. An image
from the past floated briefly before her. It was quite
irrational, the feeling she had, that made her begin
to long for some sign that he had been aware of
the strange power which had flashed between them.
It was quite different from anything she had felt
with Zak. With him it had been a kind of impatience at the game they had been playing. Now, she
realised with a shudder, there was no question of
games.

They reached the top of the tower and came out,
first Vinny, then Carlos, on to the wide flat roof
with its balustrade of ancient stones, wide as the
thickness of the walls of the tower itself, and with
enough room for a person to sit down with no fear
of plunging over the edge to the courtyard below.

Wide enough, in fact, to spread out picnic things
there, and that's exactly what an English couple
were doing now. The man was carefully setting
napkins, two glasses and a bottle of wine on top of
the level stones, while the woman was carefully
opening a box containing an elaborately decorated
gateau. It was obviously a celebration of some-

thing, an anniversary perhaps, and Vinny felt Carlos stop and look with an expression she couldn't fathom as the woman stuck the knife into the thick layers of cream. For a moment he seemed lost in thought. She herself had walked straight to the far side of the tower to gaze in wonderment at the view, and when she turned back to say something to him despite herself, she found him still looking at the couple with an expression which was almost frightening in its intensity. With a start he seemed to pull himself together as he felt her eyes on him and with a visible effort he allowed his face to relax into the now familiar self-mocking smile she had seen before.

He made his way unhurriedly to her side, and for a moment leaned out over the balustrade as if drinking in the view over the town. When he spoke his voice was hard, disparaging. 'The simple things, the simple celebrations of simple folk—how they make one's heart bleed!' He turned cold eyes on her and she felt her shoulder muscles tighten with the apprehension of some vague threat.

'Well, Vinny, forgive me for not keeping my vow of silence. But I must express my feelings when they're so moved by such a touching spectacle of married bliss.'

Vinny dragged her gaze from the hardening in his eyes, to its cause. The couple, oblivious to their effect on Carlos, were now solemnly raising their wine glasses to each other. The presence of anyone else on the tower seemed to have no importance to them. The man seemed to move his lips in an inaudible toast and the woman smiled with a look of such pure love in her face that despite herself Vinny was moved to spring to their defence.

'Why shouldn't they celebrate their love for each other?' she demanded. 'I think it's a beautiful thing to do.'

'Can married love ever be beautiful?' he retorted, his face, despite his evident attempt to control it, twisting savagely for a moment.

'Love is love,' she replied. 'I don't see that marriage can change that.'

He laughed bitterly. 'Your parents no doubt conduct their inevitable internecine warfare behind discreetly closed doors, and endeavour to preserve the English tradition of a "stiff upper lip" at all times.'

'I don't believe there is any warfare between them,' she retorted. 'They're both reasonable people and still very much in love with one another. You seem to have an extremely jaundiced view of the world.'

'Perhaps I have my reasons,' he replied, turning his back on her. She thought he was going to relapse into silence once again, but he looked at her over his shoulder with a crooked grin from which all bitterness seemed to have fled. 'Anyway, I doubt whether those two are married . . . to each other!'

He laughed shortly and began to make his way slowly over to the other side of the tower.

'Cynic!' she called after him, smiling despite herself. She watched him come to a halt at the far corner where the tower gave on to a view of the enclosed gardens and little geometric pathway bordered by clipped myrtle hedges which surrounded the foot of the building where the Alcaide had once housed his harem.

Vinny looked carefully at her guide book, but it gave no further information about who the ladies were who had spent the best part of their lives as captives in such a carefully planned pleasure garden. She walked over to stand by his side.

'I suppose given your views on Christian marriage you think the Moorish style is preferable,' she said tartly.

He turned slowly to look at her. His glance was so piercing she felt herself beginning to tense up again. 'Don't you?' he asked softly. 'To spend your days in making music and your nights in making love? What more delightful thing is man or woman made for?'

She almost stopped breathing when he carefully put out a hand and very gently slid his fingers down the long length of her hair. For a fraction of a second she felt the warmth of his fingers brush her skin, and only when he slowly let his hand drop did she release her breath with an almost audible sigh.

'Yes,' he breathed, 'what else are angels made for?'

With a sudden angry lifting of the shoulders she turned her back on him. 'You must be mad!' she scoffed. 'It's typical of a man even in this day and age to think that's all a woman wants to make her happy.' Her cheeks were flaming but with an emotion that was not all anger. She gave him a derisive glance which did nothing to quell the look of amusement which came at once into his eyes.

'I wasn't thinking only of women,' he told her. 'I rather like the idea myself of being a devotee of the twin goddesses of music and love. What more do we need in life?'

'Someone has to work to make such things possible,' she said primly. 'Somebody has to do all the unpleasant tasks. It can't all be fun and games. Society would collapse if everyone held your views.'

'So sensible for one so young,' he mocked. 'You sound like my father. "Work hard, *majo*, work before pleasure." ' The smile which always dazzled her in its sudden brilliance broke across the levels of his face, but it was tinged with bitterness. 'So he worked hard, and what has he got——?'

Vinny looked quickly at him to see why he had broken off so suddenly, but he had averted his glance and his eyes were stony as he gazed across the gardens tumbling to the terraced hillside below them.

'What has he got?' she demanded. 'Probably a lot of satisfaction. Proud of his work, proud that he's been able to provide for his family. Proud of you, his son. That seems wholly admirable to me.' She briefly pictured a grizzled old peasant standing with his arms folded, next to a smiling though prematurely aged woman dressed in black. Barefoot children were ranged on either side of the parents.

'What do you know of it?' Carlos swung back almost angrily into the attack. 'You have no idea what you are saying. I'm sorry, this is not a topic for conversation between us.' He turned abruptly towards the steps leading back to the foot of the tower and seemed just about to descend when there was the sound of voices as a group of tourists came noisily upwards towards the roof. They were mainly Spaniards, led by a striking older woman wearing large dark glasses and dressed expensively in a white silk trouser suit, but she was evidently showing some American friends the sights, for she was talking rapidly in heavily inflected English to a portly man in tartan trousers and a panama who was coming up the steps immediately behind her.

'And this, Jefferson, is absolutely the most perfect view over the city you could hope to find. I trust you've saved plenty of film. Look, see the Vega stretching to the horizon in this direction, see the city down below at the foot of the Alhambra Hill, and here, see the even more high summer palace on the twin hill with the Sierra Nevada and the Alpujarras mountains, snow-covered, rising up in grandeur to the sky.'

She paused to allow her companions to regain their breath and adjust themselves to the spectacular panorama which met their sight.

In that instant Carlos, who had stepped back behind the protecting wall round the steps, to allow the party out on to the roof, had ducked his head and before Vinny could say anything was hurrying down the steps and was already out of sight round the first bend.

Surprised at his sudden haste on seeing the tourists and also annoyed at presumably being expected to follow him, she paused and looked back at the group who were now fanning out across the roof.

Why on earth had they had such an effect on Carlos? One minute he had been nonchalantly leaning against the parapet, the next hurrying away like somebody caught redhanded. It had been when his eyes had alighted on the elegant Spanish woman that the change had come over him, observed

Vinny all of a sudden. What had it been, that fleeting look on his face? Recognition of some kind? Shock? She tensed. Had it been guilt of some kind? She looked thoughtful. Guilt? But why? Her thoughts coiled like snakes around a suspicion which she feared to examine. There was, as Jean had told her, some secret about Carlos, an overwhelming sense that he was concealing something. Vinny dully turned towards the descending steps. It was nothing to do with her. Whatever secret he had, however unwholesome, it was none of her concern. Hadn't she had enough of secrets anyhow? Enough of shadows, and of moonlight?

Moonshine, more like, she thought rancorously. What was it to her? With unwilling steps she followed in the direction Carlos had taken, down into the shadowy depths to the foot of the tower.

CHAPTER SEVEN

WHEN she reached the bottom of the tower Carlos was pacing up and down with what seemed like an attempt at nonchalance in his manner, but Vinny felt she was not deceived by it. She gave him a searching glance, but he looked away and at once started to make for the next part of the tour.

She followed as he led at a brisk pace through corridors and courtyards, until at length she was forced to call out, 'Hey, what's the hurry?' Even then he didn't slow down much but turned and beckoned to her.

'Come, this is more worth seeing.'

He had reached an arch which led out of a dark low-ceilinged hall. There was sunlight beyond. She watched as he paused for a moment framed within the arch. His tall figure, broad-shouldered and slim-hipped, was so starkly clad in black, yet against the ornate Moorish carvings which covered the wall behind him he seemed to have something of a kind of mediaeval splendour about him. There was something classic about his looks and a suggestion of great strength and rough animal grace too in his movements. Such a man, she had already noticed, turned heads in any crowd, but of this he seemed oblivious. Just as now he seemed oblivious of the effect he was creating. She felt she could only stand and drink in the lines of his form from the safety which the length of the hall afforded.

'Don't hesitate,' he called. 'Come now. Follow me!' With that he had stepped through the arch and vanished from view.

Slowly she found herself following him, anticipation gathering inside her. She knew she was being irrational, but gradually the feeling was beginning to build that whatever happened later, she would have this day with him, and it would be enough. She remembered Jean's words from the previous night. 'It was a night out, that's all, it's been enough.'

She knew she would be foolish to involve herself in anything more. He was a charming and enigmatic man of mystery, a man Ricky had called a gigolo, and he knew she, like Jean, was of wealthy parentage. She didn't have to spell it out to herself.

She would enjoy the day for whatever it brought, but she would guard against any illusions which her sudden longing would conjure up.

She approached the archway. Three shallow steps of patterned stone led round a corner. She had a sudden desire to remove her sandals and walk barefoot. She paused long enough to unbuckle the straps, then, with the sandals dangling from her fingers, she padded barefoot over the warm stone to the corner.

A sound of water splashing into a marble fountain greeted her first, then she was round the corner and standing in a small courtyard open to the skies. Somehow the sun had come out and she was immediately aware of the soft rose-coloured stone, covered in a hieroglyphic design, coming to life in the light which played over it. But central to her awareness was the sombre figure of Carlos standing quite motionless between the graceful arches of the stone canopy which formed the setting for the fountain she had heard.

He was half turned towards her as if waiting to catch a glimpse of her as she came round the corner. His handsome chiselled features were as elegant and formal as the setting in which he stood. When his dark eyes alighted on her, the smile which had before brought his features to life broke evenly across his face, dazzling her with its suddenness, so that she was stopped in her tracks and could only stare at him, her mind empty of all words, filled only with the sudden pain of a longing which he had unwittingly aroused.

His smile faded, but his eyes never left her face. As if drawn by some invisible thread, he began to walk slowly towards her. His boots of soft leather made no sound on the mosaic floor and in one silent moment he was standing in front of her.

She knew then he was going to kiss her. With a sense of the utter futility of resisting him, she raised her eyes to his. For a long moment neither of them moved. Only the sound of the water cascading into the marble bowl gave a sense of passing time. Then in one sweet movement his lips were searching for hers and she gave herself up to the swooning pleasure which his touch brought to her hungry body. It was a kiss which seemed to go on and on. There seemed to be no end to the swelling of their emotions as their mutual need seemed to carry them along into realms which for Vinny were totally unexplored.

It was with an exertion of willpower, a sense that what she was doing was standing on a threshold over which if she dared to go there would be no turning back that she tried to release herself from his arms. At once drawn to him and fighting the power which compelled her, she tried to turn her head away, to hide her lips from his pursuing ones, but even when he released her she felt bound by the very closeness of his body, the scent of his clothes, his skin, the warmth which emanated from him, wrapping them close together as if caught in actual bonds.

Carlos neither spoke nor moved when she released herself. He looked stunned, closed, shuttered. She felt drawn to look deep into the black mirrors of his eyes as if to read some truth there, but they gleamed with an expression which only seemed to mirror her own shock.

I must get away, she thought, suddenly frantic. I

must escape. I must break free.

With a sudden parting of her lips as if she was about to speak, but conscious that no sound would come, she stepped back from him and walked rapidly the length of the court to the far end where seven delicately-wrought arches led on deeper into the heart of the palace.

With scarcely a glance at the wonders of Moorish craftsmanship, the dazzling artistry of stone and water, Vinny plunged on through the long Court of the Myrtles with its two silent pools, and went on up the steps which led to the *mirador* of Elisabetta. Here she paused for breath. The view was spectacular, each little arch with which the outer wall was pierced gave on to a subtely different view over the city at the foot of the wooded hill below the palace walls.

Fighting her rising panic at the feelings which had been so casually unleashed, she gripped the worn stone balustrade and tried to bring some order to her thoughts.

How could she have let Carlos kiss her like that? How could she allow herself to feel such a turmoil of passion for a man who was a complete stranger? He was dark and dangerous and playing her for a rich little fool. What had she done? Only a few moments ago she had imagined she could be happy knowing that they would only have this day of sightseeing together. Now she was burning with an irrational, wild longing to throw herself headlong into the black depths of his soul. Was she mad? What craziness had taken hold of her? She turned, every sense alert as she heard a movement behind her.

It was Carlos. His face was expressionless, his eyes in shadow as he came up towards her. She brushed a lock of blonde hair away from her face and waited, preparing the words carefully so that there should be no mistaking her intentions.

She waited until he was about to step up on to the balcony next to her, then she turned her cool gaze down on him, and, somehow or other concealing the wild beating of her heart, she spoke.

'Don't come any nearer. I don't want you to touch me ever again.' She paused. It seemed to her as if someone else was speaking the words for her, a stranger, with a voice as cold as ice.

He made as if to answer, but she went on. 'You may think it amusing to invite yourself into my company and then to indulge in a meaningless flirtation. I've no doubt you imagine I'm going to jump into bed with you before the day is out. Unfortunately I have standards which are no doubt as bizarre to you as your apparently casual promiscuity is to me. I'm sorry you appeared to get the wrong impression from what happened a few moments ago. I don't think it can fairly be said to be due to anything I myself have either said or done. But I'm sure you understand that I don't wish you to accompany me any further.'

With that she half turned as if to dismiss him, but with one bound he was towering beside her, his face blank with astonishment.

'But, *cara*, you know it isn't like that——' he began, but she moved abruptly away and when her voice came it was high and strained.

'You don't seem to understand,' she said coldly. 'I'm telling you to leave me alone. I thought your

English was good enough for you to grasp that fact? This is a brush-off, get it?' Her eyes sparked angrily, tears making them even brighter.

'But, angel——'

'Don't call me that!' she cried vehemently.

His face had gone pale beneath the tan.

'It must be a shock to you,' she went on relentlessly, 'to find a woman who is not a willing victim to your technique of amused half-flirting detachment. Even Jean is at this moment sitting at home with an imaginary headache in the vain hope that you'll telephone her.'

'Wait a moment—of what?' he cut in, 'technique of what? What are you talking about?'

Vinny smiled grimly. 'I also know this technique too,' she told him. 'Start a discussion about anything at all and before we know it we're deep in conversation and firmly back to square one.' She laughed with amusement. 'You'll have to be smarter than that to trap me. I've said what I had to say and that's all there is to it.'

With that she pushed past him and was half-way down the steps before he could move. She turned when she got to the bottom and looked back up at him.

'Don't follow,' she hissed, 'or I shall call one of the custodians!'

With a final toss of her head she hurried out through the courtyard, all sense of direction gone, only the blind necessity to put as much distance between them as possible driving her on.

She wandered aimlessly for the next half-hour in a maze of ornate walled gardens, heavy with the scent of orange blossom and myrtle. She roamed unseeing the tranquillity of courtyards, with the sound of water falling like tears into still pools.

Carlos had not followed her after her warning, but she was ever alert for the sight of that sleek dark head and lithe masculine figure clothed in black.

At last she was calm enough to look at the map on the back of her entrance ticket and work out the direction she had taken from the Mirador of Elisabetta to her present whereabouts.

Somehow or other she found she had left the Alhambra itself and was now at the foot of the Tower of the Little Princesses. With a listlessness she tried vainly to disown she set off towards the white-walled Generalife, the summer palace of the Alcaide, pausing now and then to look at some particularly striking view which appeared between the avenues of palms, or lingering, heavy of heart, by some waterlily-covered pool where the reflection of a girl with long blonde hair floated mysteriously in the unruffled depths.

There were few other visitors in this part of the grounds and the solitude only enhanced her melancholy mood. Once, on entering a deserted avenue of yews, she heard clearly the crunch of footsteps on gravel and she tensed expectantly as a figure appeared between the sombre-coloured trees. But it was only a gardener in bright blue overalls carrying an orange can of spray and a reel of hose. When he vanished from view at the other side of the avenue, she set off with fast beating heart towards the gate of the palace itself.

She must have spent several hours roaming half-unseeing the several courts and shaded gardens—

shaded, she thought sourly, for no apparent reason, for the sun, after its brief appearance, was again hidden behind a bank of cloud.

She had noticed earlier, without much interest, that the distant Alpujarras which the Spanish woman on the tower had pointed out to her guests had become obscured under a fine haze, and it was only now, as she stood near the summit of the Generalife, that she realised the significance of this. In single drops at first, then in twos and threes, and finally in a heavy drenching curtain of water, the rain had swiftly locked the palace in its grasp.

With an exclamation of dismay Vinny had looked round frantically for shelter. But the thick dark leaves of the palms fanned straight upwards and there seemed to be no alternative but to walk back, head held high, defying the fact that in almost no time at all her cotton jacket was soaking wet and her skirt was flapping in damp uncomfortable folds across her knees with each step she took.

She cursed herself for not thinking to bring a raincoat, but after a time she began to enjoy her battle with the elements with a sort of defiant, savage triumph.

'Bloody, bold and undefeated, here march I!' she began to sing, delighting suddenly in the freedom of the deserted road as it wound, shining now and gushing with water, towards the golden walls of the Alhambra.

Somehow it seemed fitting that the tears which she knew were bottled up inside her should have some actual counterpart in nature, and she was singing at the top of her voice by the time she reached the deserted exit.

Jean's mother was not a little put out when the wet and dishevelled girl eventually drove up to the villa in Jean's sports car.

Too tactful to say much, she had merely commented on the suddeness of the downpour, and when Vinny had offered no explanation as to why she had failed to take proper shelter, she had merely offered the information that *tapas* would be served shortly in the dining room.

'*Tapas?*' queried Vinny. She had lost all sense of time, simply observing that the shops in town had mainly seemed to be shut as she went to pick up the car.

'We always mark the end of siesta with a light snack,' explained Mrs Cotton. 'As dinner is usually taken so late it makes sense to eat the main meal of the day in the cool of the evening. *Tapas* bridge the long gap between lunch and dinner.'

Vinny looked astonished. 'I'd no idea it was so late!' she exclaimed. 'I must have missed lunch entirely.' She looked concerned. 'Jean must have been worried about her car. Did she want to use it herself this afternoon?'

Mrs Cotton smiled. 'No, I don't think so. She's ensconced in the music-room with a pile of old records. I think she's going somewhere special tonight as there's been quite a hair-washing session all afternoon.'

'I'll go and join her,' grinned Vinny, expressing a momentary lightheartedness which she knew she did not really feel.

Just then the phone shrilled and Mrs Cotton went to answer it.

'Hi, sweety!' called Jean from the doorway. 'I thought I heard voices. Manage to get the car all right?'

'Yes. Sorry I'm late back,' replied Vinny.

'You must have had a good day,' Jean went on without waiting for explanations. 'And haven't I got something to tell you!'

She went back into the room, beckoning for Vinny to follow her, but before she could do so Mrs Cotton called from the sitting-room.

'For you, Vinny. A call from England.'

'For me?' Vinny's heart fluttered with apprehension and she flew to take up the receiver. Who on earth could be calling all the way from England unless it was something terribly urgent? Had something dreadful happened while she'd been away?

With her heart in her mouth she spoke nervously into the mouthpiece.

'Hello, darling, are you missing me?' drawled a familiar boyish voice. Her fears were allayed at once.

'Zak? Is that you?' She wrinkled her forehead. 'I thought you were supposed to be in Italy?'

'I'm back,' he told her. 'In fact I'm ringing from your house, so this will have to be quick as they don't know I'm still here.'

'What?' She furrowed her brow. This sounded suspicious. What on earth was he up to? 'Why don't they know you're there?'

'They seem to be entertaining a few friends from the hunting fraternity. I gather I'm persona non grata. But we don't want to waste precious minutes talking about all that. I've decided to come and see you.'

'Wait a moment. Is Mother there?'

His voice was insinuating. 'Surely you'd rather talk to me?'

'Zak——' Vinny's voice was suddenly sharper. 'Are you ringing from the phone in the cloak-room?'

'Yes. Why?' He sounded wary.

'I see.' Vinny paused.

'Vinny, don't be so stuffy.'

Her eyes were thoughtful. The cloakroom was just off the main entrance. It was a small room where the muddy boots and raincoats were kept. It was handy to have a phone installed there. It was also very private. Unless someone happened to pick up an extension in the house and found it engaged, there was little chance of anyone knowing about Zak's call. Vinny felt a surge of annoyance that Zak should make so free with her parents' hospitality. At the same time she was perturbed by her own uncharacteristic churlishness when he had bothered to make so romantic a gesture.

Stifling her annoyance, she asked casually, 'Why are you back so soon?'

'Uncle was being a bit of a bore,' Zak told her with a note of peevishness in his voice which she had never detected before. 'He just wanted a chauffeur without the expense. I wasted most of my time just sitting around in his car while he visited old flames. Do you know——' he went on, 'I didn't get to see any paintings and he didn't even offer me an allowance. *And* I had to eat in the hotel all the time.'

'I thought he was staying with friends?'

'*He* was. But they foisted me off at some third-rate *pensione* in the village. I had to report for driving duties like a common cabby each morning while he and his friends lived it up. I was thoroughly bored and insulted. In fact, I've never been so humiliated in all my life——' His voice rose to a squeak of anger, and Lavinia held the phone away as he continued.

'All in all——' he was saying, 'I've had a thoroughly rotten summer. And to cap it all, when I rushed back hoping to find you waiting for me, I discovered that even *you* had deserted me. Imagine how I feel!'

Zak's tone of voice left Vinny in doubt. But before she had a chance to say anything he was going on again.

'My one stroke of luck,' he was telling her,' was to notice a letter from you to your mother on the bureau as I was leaving. I thought if I set off tomorrow morning I can be with you by the end of the week——'

'You mean you opened a letter addressed to my mother——!' But again Zak ignored her and carried straight on.

'I'd like to see the Prado really—pity you're in Granada. But we can do the galleries in Madrid on our way back to England. You do have the use of a car, I suppose? No matter if not. You can always hire one. We'll share the driving between us.' He paused. 'Vinny? Are you still there?'

Vinny took a deep breath and her voice was steady when she at last spoke.

'Zak, I think you've forgotten something. I'm

here to work. I intend to stay for the full term of
my contract. I shan't be doing any sightseeing for
some time.'

'That's all right,' he told her amiably. 'I've got
quite a taste for café life and I've nothing to come
back here for.'

'But where do you intend to stay for the next
two months?' she asked casually.

'With you, of course,' he said, in a voice full of
surprise. 'Where else, my darling?'

'Zak,' she interrupted, 'I really don't think this
is a good idea——'

'Sorry?'

Was he pretending to be stupid, she wondered,
or did he really not understand? As if to a child,
which indeed he was, she thought, she tried to spell
it out. 'I happen to be staying with friends of one
of my brother's friends. We haven't known each
other long enough for me to take liberties with their
hospitality. I suppose you think that's stuffy of me
too. However, it's not on for you to stay here.'

There was a pause at the other end. 'You love
me, don't you?' The voice was sulky. 'You're
supposed to love me, aren't you?'

The abruptness of the question made Vinny
hesitate. 'Listen, Zak, I don't know what I feel right
now. I just don't think you can invite yourself to
stay——' She thought rapidly. 'I can't ask them to
put you up. There's no room, apart from anything
else.'

'It must be a huge place. And you know me, any
old room will do. Put me in the attic, I don't care.'

Vinny felt manipulated. Now she was supposed
to feel sorry for him—poor homeless waif. Instead

she felt a sudden spurt of anger.

'Listen to me. It's not just a question of a room. It's—it's the whole thing.'

But before she could try to explain how her feelings had changed he said: 'Listen, there's someone outside the door. Leave it till we meet. I'll set off tomorrow, then we can talk it out when I see you. Phones are a damnable invention anyway.'

'Wait! Zak, wait!' she almost screeched down the phone, and for a moment she thought he had already hung up. 'Are you still there? Listen to me!'

She heard him mutter something about making it snappy and the sense of urgency made her come abruptly to the point.

'It's not going to work,' she told him emphatically. 'No way will it work. I'm sorry, I don't want to see you. I doubt whether I'll want to see you again. It's over. And I'm truly sorry to have to tell you like this, but—Zak? Are you still there?'

He said he was. His voice was peevish.

Now she suddenly saw the relationship very clearly, and the words seemed to come more easily than she had ever expected. It was like waking from a bad dream.

She said: 'We may as well get it straight now. Because I don't want you to be in any doubt about what I'm saying. It's the whole thing from beginning to end. I'm sick of your assumption that everyone's around for your sole benefit. I'm sick of your sly little half-smiles when you see somebody fall into line with your plans. I went along with it for so long because I just didn't believe anybody could be so calculating, so devious, so

single-minded in organising everything and everyone to suit themselves. I was so blinded by infatuation that I just didn't see it until now. But now I
can see clearly. And I can see you do that sort of
thing all the time. And I'm sick and tired of it. So
there. It makes me sick. And if you think for one
minute you can do your usual trick of trying to
soft talk me into—hello? Are you still there?'

There came the distant sound of voices raised in
anger than the familiar tones of her mother's voice
came over the line.

'Vinny? That's the most sensible decision you've
ever made, my darling.'

'Mummy? Oh, Mummy. . . .' For no reason at
all Vinny felt her bottom lip begin to quiver. The
misery of the last few hours had driven her to say
things which had for a long time been buried in
the most secret recesses of her heart. Now she felt
drained.

'Darling, are you all right? Is everything all right
there?'

'Yes, oh yes. . . .' She paused and took a deep
gulping breath. 'It's all very—interesting.' She bit
her lip. Everything *would* be all right. It wasn't
quite a lie. Things would sort themselves out now.
Now she had made a start at sorting herself out.

'Zak, I may as well tell you, has just been shown
the door by Derek, but not, I regret to say, without
first having a bottle of your father's best Scotch
removed from his pocket.'

'Oh now, really!' Vinny was appalled. So they
had been right all along. Her outburst just now
had not been misplaced.

'I really am sorry, Mummy.'

'It's not your fault, my dear. He's a very plausible young man. I only hope you won't be foolish again. Especially as you're so far from home.'

'Never fear—I won't make the same mistake twice.' Vinny's chin rose. She felt quite composed by the time she came to hand the receiver over to Mrs Cotton so that the two mothers could have a word together, and it was with the kind of sigh that comes after a particularly nasty but necessary piece of work has been done that she turned towards the music-room.

Jean was still hanging around the half-opened door, but her eagerness was not due to a desire to hear Vinny's news, but to something she wanted to tell Vinny about herself. There was an air of ill-concealed excitement about the younger girl's movements as she made sure the door was firmly closed behind them.

Then straightaway she turned to Vinny with shining eyes.

'Guess what!' she demanded.

'I'm not good at guessing games, so you may as well tell me straight off,' laughed Vinny, glad to have some immediate relief from the turmoil of her own thoughts. She waited.

'*I*'ve had a phone call too,' said Jean, giving a hurried glance towards the door. She lowered her voice. 'Can you guess who from?'

Icy fingers seemed to run up and down Vinny's spine at her words. 'From Ricky?' she breathed hopefully, fear tugging at her. She looked searchingly into Jean's flushed face. She knew even before the girl spoke his name, that her fears were justified. She turned away, but Jean came up behind her.

'You'll think I'm mad feeling this way about someone like that. But I just can't help it. He's asked me to go to the Club again tonight, as his guest. He's been booked to play the whole week.'

'Then what?' asked Vinny harshly. 'Where's he going after that?'

'Who knows?' replied Jean, the smile momentarily leaving her face. 'But who cares? I'm not looking for anything permanent. I don't mind being a one-night stand.' She paused. 'I suppose you think that's cheap? I don't. I want him. And I'm going to have him.'

She picked up the hair-dryer and set its controls.

'I'm inviting Ricky too, just to allay Mum's suspicions. I know you won't mind using your charms a little in that direction. After all,' she switched on the dryer, 'what else are friends for? You know I'd do the same for you.'

CHAPTER EIGHT

As it happened Vinny managed to cry off the invitation to Curro's. It was easily done. She had to be up early the next morning for her first day at the school and Jean, not without a small moue of disappointment, had to accept the common sense of this decision.

'Oh well, Ricky will just have to play gooseberry,' she said with a shrug of her shoulders. 'I

guess it's his own look-out if he decides to put up
with me after this.'

Vinny nodded dully. She couldn't bring herself
to care one way or the other what the two of them
got up to, she was still unable to shake off her
irrational sense of something lost.

Dragging herself out of bed next morning with
the alarm still ringing in her ears, she resolved to
take herself in hand, and with an effort she began
to argue herself into a more positive frame of
mind.

The phone call from Zak, disturbing though it
had been, had somehow cleared the air, and now
more immediate worries seemed to press in on her.
Somehow she could not shake off a terrible sense
of loss—but it wasn't for the English boy. On the
contrary—and she knew this without the shadow
of a doubt—it was for the Spaniard, the man who
was almost a stranger, yet whose kisses burned in
her memory with a terrible fire.

How could she imagine she felt loss for something she had never really had? Carlos was nothing
but a passing stranger. He had flirted briefly with
her, as men often did, perhaps hoping it would lead
on to something else, but with no promise of anything wonderful. It was silly. There was no good
reason for her present state of turmoil. On the
contrary, life was for the moment planned and
predictable. There would be a certain amount of
challenge in taking the first step in her career. She
must rid herself of cobwebby romantic illusions
and bring all her energies to the new job ahead of
her.

But even as she brushed her hair and pinned it

up into a sleek blonde knot on top of her head, she knew she had and always would have a romantic streak which must one day find satisfaction in the real workaday world. One day she would find a nice sensible man who, like her, harboured secret dreams of romantic love. And when they met, perhaps in some mundane place, on a crowded London tube, or in some busy office, they would know each other by some hidden sign, and a flash of recognition would pass between them.

She shuddered. It would be something like the power that had shaken her so much the previous day—but this time the man would be possible, in all respects a sensible choice.

'Buenos dias!' Luisa, Mrs. Cotton's maid, tapped lightly on the bedroom door. 'Mrs Cotton says it is now the time to leave.'

Vinny came abruptly out of her fantasising. Here she was, on the first day, dreaming away the precious minutes when she should be concentrating on getting out in time. She shook herself. What a start! She flung on a cardigan, picked up a pile of books, and made her way briskly down to breakfast.

As she walked into the dining-room she noticed at once that there was no sign of Jean.

As Mrs Cotton poured coffee she remarked on this and the older woman looked momentarily worried. 'She came crawling in not long ago,' she answered rather severely. 'I expect she'll spend the rest of the day in bed again.' She shot a searching glance at Vinny. 'I gather you met this boy Ricky the other evening?' she said.

'Yes,' replied Vinny cautiously.

'What type is he?' queried Mrs Cotton, carefully

pouring cream on to the back of a silver spoon and letting it swirl thickly over the coffee.

'Very nice,' replied Vinny truthfully. 'I think you'd like him.' She paused, and added, 'He's American. His family are quite wealthy, so I gather. His father's some sort of high-up with the German branch of an international chemical company, but I forget which.'

Mrs Cotton seemed to relax. 'It looks as if we'd better invite the boy to dinner soon, then.' She sipped her coffee without further comment.

Vinny felt ashamed of the small deceit she had practised in order to save Jean's skin. It was obviously her daughter's late night which had given rise to Mrs Cotton's questions and Vinny knew that if a single word had been breathed about Jean's actual escort, the serene expression which Mrs Cotton's face now wore would have been wiped away in an instant.

Vinny's first day passed interestingly enough. It was a small school and her classes were groups of no more than ten students, many of whom were housewives with one or two businessmen who needed to acquire a smattering of commercial English for export reasons.

The day was split up into two with a session in the morning and another after the long afternoon break, and she felt pleasantly taxed by the time eight o'clock came round and it was time to set off back to the villa.

There had been, she noted wryly, no magic flash of recognition between her or anyone else among the staff or students, though everyone was pleasant enough and she knew her ash blonde good-looks had a definite appeal.

She set her face grimly, determined to keep to her resolve to have no truck with romantic fantasies for the time being. When she got back to the villa, dinner was already being prepared, and she wondered, with not a little trepidation, how she would be able to face Jean's no doubt graphic account of her night with Carlos once the meal was over. But to her surprise Jean did not appear at dinner, and Mrs Cotton looked apologetic.

'I'm afraid Jean has already left,' she told Vinny. 'She said to tell you they would be at some club in town—C—C——'

'Curro's?' supplied Vinny with a sinking heart.

'Curro's, yes. Is it a nice place?' asked Mrs Cotton, furrowing her brow.

'I can't say I've ever heard it mentioned. I thought we knew the names of most of the night clubs in town.'

'It's not really a night club' explained Vinny, 'and it's only small.'

'I gather it's for *aficionados* of flamenco,' queried Mrs Cotton. 'I do hope it's not a dive.'

Vinny, despite the leaden feeling in her heart, smiled at this word. 'It doesn't look very swish, I must admit, but it's where the students all go.'

'Ah, students,' Mrs Cotton frowned. Then she looked up with a smile. 'I suppose it's all right if Ricky is with her. I've asked her to invite him over to dinner at the weekend. And to bring a friend. We can have quite a little party. I do like to keep in touch with her friends.'

Vinny listened without really hearing. She knew

that if she breathed a word of Jean's doings she could stop her seeing Carlos in an instant. Instead she repeated her assurances about Ricky's undoubted suitability, but again declined the invitation to meet Jean and her escort at the club. She felt justified in keeping Mrs Cotton in the dark with the knowledge that El Brasiliano would be moving on by the end of the week anyway, then no doubt Jean would return to normal.

'I must say,' remarked Mrs Cotton, you're looking rather wan. I think you're wise to have an early night again.' She nodded approvingly. And Vinny spent the rest of the evening recounting her day's doing and making some pretence at swotting up on her Spanish.

It was with relief that she eventually retired to the privacy of her own room and climbed into bed.

It was another sleepless night. But this time she did hear Jean's little car purring up the steep drive to the villa, and, irrationally, once she knew Jean was home, she turned on her side and fell asleep at once.

The next two or three days passed in similar fashion, Vinny leaving for the school before Jean was up, and returning shortly after she had already gone out again. On the second day there was a note in her room saying: 'El Suizo's tomorrow at 2 and keep Saturday free, signed, ecstatically yours, Jean,' and on the third day was a picture postcard of the nearby glacier in the Sierra with the cryptic note, 'And it didn't melt!'

Mrs Cotton made no more reference to Jean's late nights, presumably thinking that her sudden passion for flamenco music would burn itself out as her involvement with the American boy increased. Vinny simply put all her energies into teaching and getting the beginnings of a respectable sun tan now that the weather had taken a turn for the better.

She would go out on to the roof of the school building when the morning session ended and stay there nicely browning until the beginning of the afternoon session. She had neither the energy nor the inclination to gather with the other teachers in one of the bars down town, and she assiduously avoided any idea of taking coffee in El Suizo's for fear of whom she might meet there.

It was on the Friday when, dragging herself wearily across the square to the bus stop, with not a little satisfaction at having completed her first week successfully, she heard a familiar voice call her name.

She turned just as a black-clad figure detached itself from the shadow of a nearby building and came striding towards her.

Her heart leapt at once into her mouth. Good resolutions crumbled to dust and her back stiffened in a spirit of self-preservation as she prepared to run.

'Momento!' he gripped her fiercely by the shoulder as she turned away.

'Ouch! You're hurting me!' She struggled frantically, not caring what the passersby were thinking, but Carlos only tightened his grip.

'Keep still, then,' he told her grimly. 'I want a word with you.'

She stood still then, tensed and ready for flight.

'I want to speak with you.' His face seemed grim and she waited, breathing hard with anger for him to go on.

He hesitated and before he could speak she couldn't resist saying cuttingly: 'No doubt you want me to pass a message for Jean?'

He shrugged. 'I shall see her this evening in Curro's no doubt. Any message can wait till then surely. Why do you say such a thing?'

Vinny compressed her lips and gazed stonily into the distance.

'I'm in rather a hurry. I've had a tiring week and want to get home as soon as possible so that I can have a shower and a bite to eat. Would you mind telling me what it is you have to say and then letting me go?'

A tremor passed over his tanned features before he spoke.

'I've no intention of saying what I have to say in the middle of a public thoroughfare. You'll come with me to somewhere more private.'

'I shall not!' burst out Vinny.

'Oh, but you shall!' He put his arm round her waist and began to march her along the street. She struggled, but it only made him tighten his grip. There was a smile on his face when he bent to whisper a warning in her ear. 'If you continue to fight I shall have no choice but to pick you up in my arms and carry you like a baby.'

'You just try it!' she spat.

'Then come quietly. I'm not going to rape you. I just want a few quiet words.'

'I don't see why you can't say what you want to say here,' muttered Vinny weakly, knowing that she would go with him despite herself.

'You'll find out soon enough,' was his reply as he slackened his painful hold on her forearm. 'Now be a good girl and come along.'

'You realise you're practically kidnapping me?' she asked as they walked along, looking to any casual passerby almost amicable, with his arm still round her waist.

'I know,' he told her, 'I've been planning it all week. I haven't yet worked out how much ransom I'm going to ask. Something exorbitant, in the hope that no one can pay.'

She felt a sudden nag of fear. Underneath his bantering tone, could he be speaking the truth? Did he really believe she was an heiress of some sort? Kidnappings were common these days.

'You wouldn't get much for me. My people are as poor as church mice,' she told him, not altogether truthfully.

He looked at her with a sardonic smile. 'Poor, rich, what does it mean? I don't think you, in your beautiful, expensive clothes, know what it is to be poor.'

She tried to draw back from him, her nerves beginning to sound an alarm of fear, but they were already at the entrance to the seedy hotel Carlos had pointed out to her the day they had gone up to the Alhambra and before she could loosen his hold, he had pulled her into the dark entrance hall and was already sliding back the old-fashioned lift doors which faced them. As she stumbled over the threshold she turned quickly and tried to duck out of his reach.

'No!' she exclaimed. 'Let me go!' She saw his

game now and cursed herself for being such a trusting fool. How could she have allowed herself to be brought here by an almost complete stranger? God knows what sort of story he had picked up about her from Jean, but that had obviously helped him to make up his mind where the richest pickings were to be made. When he discovered the truth who knew what he would do to her.

His black bulk completely blocked the exit, and Vinny fought and spat like a wildcat to prevent him swinging the heavy cage door shut, but though her actions took him by surprise, her strength was no match for his, and after the initial shock had worn off, he managed to push her into the corner long enough to slam the doors shut and press the button to ascend.

In a wild panic she flung herself towards the emergency bell, but again he was too quick for her, and her fingers slid harmlessly down the panel with his strong fingers digging hurtfully into her wrist.

'Let me go, you monster!' she cried. 'I shall scream the place down!' And she took a deep breath and opened her mouth to scream, but before she could make any sound Carlos had crushed her body to his and his lips were bruisingly covering her own while one of his hands searched for a firm grip on either side of her jaw. When he was sure she could neither breath because of the pressure with which he held her to him, nor move her jaw because he held it in a vice, he removed his lips from hers and darkly threatened her with worse punishment if she should dare to raise her voice above a whisper.

The pain in her jaw was increased to let her know

who was momentarily boss, and with tears of anger and frustration in her eyes she weakly nodded her assent.

He seemed to believe her, for he at once let her go, even going so far as to straighten her collar for her and pick up her bag where it had fallen in the scuffle. Vinny was too frightened to speak and waited, feeling like a lamb going to the slaughter, until the lift stopped, the gates were flung open, and, with a curt nod, Carlos gestured that she should get out.

They were on the fourth or fifth floor—she had lost count—and came out into a small vestibule, with traditional tiled floor and walls of dark brown peeling paper, with great chunks of stucco missing from the frieze around the windows. There was a distinct smell of boiled cabbage, and as he ushered her forward into a narrow passageway, she could see a line of rather grubby-looking washing draped across from window to window in the space between the ventilation shaft.

He took a large key from his pocket with his left hand, his other being still tight around her waist, and managed to push open the door without letting go of her.

Inside it was quite what Vinny had expected, though somewhat smaller. Again the floor was tiled in the traditional Spanish fashion, and the walls could have done with a fresh coat of paint. A bed dominated the room and apart from a cheap wooden cupboard, its door jammed shut with a wedge of paper, this was the only piece of furniture there was. A washbasin took up one corner and some shaving tackle was lined up on a shelf below a small cracked mirror. Finally, covering almost all of one wall, was a huge black and white close-up of El Cordobes, the matador. Vinny saw at once that unless they were to have their conversation while standing up, there would be nowhere to sit but on the bed. All this she noticed in the instant which it took Carlos to push her into the room and lock the door behind them.

She watched him pocket the key. He must have noticed the scornful expression on her face, for he raised his eyebrows questioningly.

'Not content with demonstrating that you're much stronger than me,' she derided, 'you even have to hammer the point home that I'm temporarily in your power, by actually locking the door.'

'I assure you,' he said, with a suggestion of sharpness in his tone, 'I'm not locking the door in order to show who's boss, but merely in order to keep it shut properly. It has a nasty habit of coming open. Look.' He unlocked the door and immediately it swung open. 'Satisfied?'

Vinny tossed her head. He locked the door again, flung the key ostentatiously on to the bed, then went to sit on the windowsill on the other side of the room.

'Sit if you want,' he indicated the bed.

'I'll stand.'

'As you wish.' He sighed and closed his eyes for a moment.

Vinny had time to notice that instead of the threadbare jacket and trousers of previous occasions, he was wearing a long-sleeved sweat-shirt and a pair of well-fitting drill jeans. Both were, of course, black, as were his leather boots.

She suddenly realised he was looking at her, a quizzical kind of smile on his face. There was a look in his eyes too which set her thoughts racing.

'Lavinia,' he said at last, 'I don't want it to be like this.' He paused for a moment. 'It's difficult to know where to begin.' He paused again.

She couldn't resist the opportunity to say, 'How intriguing to find the great Brasiliano at a loss for words!' Her tone was derisive.

'Yes, it would amuse you,' he said quietly.

'I must say I've been quite overwhelmed by your command of English so far,' she went on. 'You must have had excellent teachers.'

'The English themselves,' he told her. 'I was at Eton for a while.' She must have let her disbelief show for he went on, 'I didn't bring you here to spin you a yarn.'

She waited, letting him speak.

'Fate seems to have thrown us together. I believe in fate. I believe we're meant to take notice when it tries to tell us something. The day I saved you from falling in front of that train was no accident. I'd been watching you as you walked along the platform. You were like a beautiful vision—I couldn't take my eyes off you. When you drew level with me I had just decided that I must pull myself together and stop behaving like an infatuated schoolboy. Then you did that stupid thing. It was easy for me to be ready. I acted without thinking. I'm not asking for gratitude. I'm not trying to revive memories of something you'd no doubt rather forget.' He paused.

Vinny took the opportunity to draw herself up and ask: 'Look, where is this leading us? What do you want with me?' Ideas of herself as his kidnap victim were slowly receding.

Carlos turned away and looked out of the window at the panorama of tiled roofs on the other side of the street. 'What do I want with you? It's too soon to say.' His voice was subdued, and when he turned back to face her there was a softer gleam in his eyes, the import of which Vinny tried valiantly to ignore.

'I believe fate meant us to meet. I believe we were both wrong to turn away from it. That's why we were given a second chance that night outside the club. But again, something went wrong.'

'You spent the entire evening paying attention to someone else. That's what went wrong,' Vinny said sharply before she could stop herself.

'Ah!' He threw back his head and smiled at her through eyes that sparkled. 'Dear Jean. She's a sweet girl, but, how would you say, rather pushy?'

'That's not very loyal, considering you've spent the last three nights with her!'

'I?' Carlos looked shocked.

Vinny laughed, scornfully. 'We do happen to live in the same house, you know. I'm fully aware that she hasn't been getting home much before dawn this week. You needn't deny it.'

Carlos looked inscrutable and he didn't reply for a moment or two. When he spoke there was an edge to his voice. 'Will you believe me if I say she was not with me except on that first night as my guest? You were invited also; but you didn't turn up.' He ran fingers briefly through his thick dark hair.

Vinny looked with disdainful amusement at the

confusion of his handsome face, now even more rakishly good-looking as a lock of hair fell forward on to his brow.

'You must think me very stupid,' she said coldly. 'Of course I shan't believe you.'

'That's fair enough,' he said after a pause. 'There's no reason why you should until you've had my words confirmed by Jean herself.'

Vinny stopped short. 'Very well,' she said at length, 'that's a deal. I'll believe you if it'll give you any satisfaction, when what you say is corroborated by Jean.' There, she thought, that will call his bluff. She looked steadily back at him. 'Now what?'

Carlos got down from his lounging perch on the windowsill and came towards her. '*Cara*, let's start again. Let's be kinder to each other.'

'Kind?' Vinny took a step backwards.

'*Dios!*' He ran his fingers through his hair again. 'This language! Am I not making myself clear? I want to see you, be with you, talk to you, hold you in my arms like that time in the palace. I want to get to know you as fate seems to have decreed. Is that plain enough?'

He stood before her, challenging a response.

Vinny gave a shaky laugh. 'But this is ridiculous!' she replied, standing her ground. 'We would have, so I understand, about two days in which to do all this before you set out upon your travels again. Do you really think that's sufficient time to do as fate decrees?'

'A lifetime would not be long enough—but I can see you're determined to mock me. What are you afraid of? Your eyes tell a different story.' He moved closer. 'Angel, give me one night.'

'As I thought I'd made clear before, I don't go in for that sort of thing. But I'll say one thing for you, you're persistent.' She made as if to turn to the door.

'Wait! All roads lead back to Granada as long as you are here. If I have to fulfil engagements in other cities that doesn't mean that we cannot pursue our relationship.'

'I don't fancy being your Granada stop-over,' she said cuttingly.

'That's not what I intend!' he flashed back.

Vinny gave a hard laugh. 'Will you please unlock this door and let me go?'

'If I say no?' His face was set in an expression which would have frightened her if she hadn't been in such a towering passion at the import of his words. She fumed at him without speaking. Their mutual anger was an almost tangible force in the room.

'Sit down! Now!'

She felt her muscles stiffen at the power in his tone, but she didn't budge.

'Sit or I'll make you!' Carlos said again through clenched teeth. 'You are going to listen to me!'

He came towards her and grabbing her by the shoulders forced her down on to the bed. For a moment she was tempted to fight back, to bite and kick and scratch in pure self-defence, but fearing his superior strength and the sudden cold anger which suffused his face, she submitted to his will without a word, only wrapping her arms tightly round her knees while lying motionless where he had pushed her.

'There is something you have to understand. I

am a musician.' He began to pace the room, covering the space between the bed and the window in only two or three strides before turning back again to where she lay on the bed. He kept looking at her to make sure she followed what he was trying to say. Somehow his English seemed to acquire a more Spanish intonation, as if the emotion with which his words were imbued made him temporarily lose his usual control over the language.

'My life,' he began, 'is not one of comfort and predictability. My future is uncertain. One thing is sure, however—I have to follow the path laid down for me without wavering from it. A flamenco player of necessity leads what to outsiders must appear to be a life of great irregularity. We work when respectable citizens sleep. We receive, too, excessive adoration from the public——' he smiled dryly. 'That does not mean that we ourselves feel an equivalent adoration towards the particular individuals who claim to feel such things for us. Do you understand this?'

Vinny shrugged as best she could with her hands still wrapped round her knees, and shut her eyes, refusing to give him the encouragement of seeing what was in them. He turned back and did another turn across the room and back.

'Listen, do you know the Spanish word *duende*?'

Vinny opened her eyes but did not answer.

'I don't know an exact equivalent in English. The dictionary says something like spirit, or fairy, but it's more than that, much more.' Carlos heaved a sigh. 'I don't even know whether you're listening to this.'

She raised her head. 'Of course I'm listening,' she told him. 'It's the most roundabout way anybody has ever tried to get me into bed before. I'm utterly fascinated.'

He laughed bitterly. 'If that's all I wanted I could take you now,' he told her. 'There's no one within earshot, and anyway, they expect me to make a bit of a noise in my lovemaking, being such a disreputable character.'

He came over to the bed and sat down beside her. 'Listen carefully, *cara*, I'm going to try to explain something to you. Whether or not you walk out of here determined never to see me again will be entirely up to you. But something, fate, call it what you will, compels me to say these things to you. So, as the phrase is: here goes.'

CHAPTER NINE

'I'LL tell you about a conversation I had with my father a long time ago,' Carlos began. 'He was a man who had only one god—Mammon. If a thing could not be bought and sold, he was not interested in it. He hated my playing, my singing. He said to me: You can play in your spare time, play the guitar if you must, it's a nice hobby, play, he said, to entertain your friends. Entertain?' Carlos looked down into Vinny's face to see if she understood. 'Art is not mere entertainment. Flamenco is not just a jolly way in which to pass the time. It's an ancient and exacting art form. It brings us close to the gods. I tried to tell him this—me, eighteen, very unsure of my talent, still a little in awe of this——' he paused, 'this man, my father.' He looked questioning. 'You nearly smile?'

'Yes,' she said. 'You? Unsure of your talent?'

'It was some years ago. I was a boy,' he replied with a hint of a smile. 'However, this is the point. A city like Granada—oh, any city, they are full of amateurs, amateur this and that, would-be painters, musicians, writers, actors, singers, dancers. Have you noticed how many amateur poets there are in El Suizo's? They are third-raters, all of them, halfhearted in their commitment. They don't understand what they are dabbling in. They are in love with themselves and without passion for their art. I tried to explain this. I said—this youth, eighteen—I said: Don't you realise that the Muses are goddesses? Angels? That when a singer of flamenco takes the boards the dark angel spreads her wings, the dark angel of *duende*, and she demands total allegiance? She demands the life blood of all those who presume to be her servants. Where she leads, I must follow. I have no choice in this. To be an artist is a life or death matter. It demands one's soul.'

His face had taken on an ethereal, abstract quality, as if the boy whose words he was remembering still lived inside the body of the mature man.

Vinny felt herself move into a crouching position in front of him. The room seemed very still.

Carlos gave a crooked smile. 'And that old man, he said: Make this your hobby.' He gave a short laugh.

'What happened then?' asked Vinny quietly. 'Did he finally come to see that you have to be a singer?'

Carlos' face twisted with some unspoken pain and he turned his head. His voice was controlled and exact when he finally spoke.

'He threw me out. I went to South America.' He looked quickly back at Vinny with a grin. 'Now I'm home—and we shall see, eh?'

'Has he heard you play since you came back?'

'Dear angel, when a Spanish father throws out his only son, things are serious. One does not immediately issue invitations to one another. When the time is right, who knows?' he swung down off the bed. 'I've said all this to try to show you that although we will sometimes not be able to spend much time together, I am serious about you. I want to see you whenever possible. What is that admirable English phrase: I want us to play it by ear—is that right?'

Vinny smiled. 'I'll say this for you, you're a damned plausible devil.'

To confirm this judgment he gave her one of his sudden devilish grins and, coming straight over to the bed, he pulled her up to standing and took her tenderly in his arms. 'My sweet love,' he said, brushing his lips against her temple, 'is this your answer? If it is, it gives me hope.'

She looked up at him, unable to conceal her total capitulation to the urgency of his demands. 'I am no heiress,' she felt constrained to tell him.

'Heiress?' He looked genuinely puzzled.

'I have no money,' she said bluntly.

'Well, you are a student of Spanish language.

What student has money? I don't follow?'

She looked bewildered. 'No, I'm not a student. I teach. My job here—my job is to teach English.'

Carlos laughed. 'So, I got it wrong. Jean said you were getting up early to go to the language school. I automatically assumed that your daddy had packed you off to Spain to learn the language. So what? You have no money. Neither have I! Who cares about that? We'll do as the peasants do and live on love and roses.'

Then he brought his longed-for lips gently but insistently down on to hers and she was lost in the surging joy of his embrace.

It was only the sound of footsteps along the passageway that brought Vinny with a jolt into the real world again. Her body stiffened slightly and Carlos, whose ardour had been increasing to the point where there would soon be no turning back, responded to her movement with a slight lifting of his head. His voice was hoarse with emotion when he spoke.

'*Cariña,*' he breathed, 'we must stop ourselves going too far.'

Despite his words she felt her body mould itself to his and her lips searched for him with an even more insistent fire.

'No——' He held her undulating body tightly against his as if to calm her, but the heat of his body only served to increase her desire. She opened her eyes, beseeching him to give her the strength to control her wild longing, and with a groan of anguish he thrust her to one side and leaned back against the door. He closed his eyes and his face, despite its bronze, seemed pale with the effort of battling with the power of their shared desire. She retreated a little from him, breathing hard, her fists clenching on their sudden loss. 'I'd better go.' Her voice was scarcely audible.

He opened his eyes. 'I'll come out with you.' He let a long breath drain the tension from his body and when he looked at her again, his eyes were bright with emotion. 'My intention was to let you go away to think about what a relationship with me would mean,' he told her with a crooked grin. 'I have little to offer. I won't even be able to see you for long stretches of time, but I never expected this——' he waved a hand as if to indicate the almost tangible presence of their desire. 'It seems already to be a sufficient answer.' He looked searchingly into her face. 'Please be certain, my darling. Don't rush.'

Vinny still felt the shudders of an unrequited need through every newly awakened nerve. It was with an effort that she tried to find the words which would express to him the turmoil of emotions he had aroused. At length she said, 'My mind is made up. I don't care about the obstacles in our way. We can overcome them somehow or other.' She smiled across the cheap hotel room, oblivious to the squalor around them.

'Come now,' he said. 'If we stay here we shall do something we may both afterwards regret. I want our first time, every time, to be beautiful, as befits our feelings. I must eat also, and then prepare myself for tonight's performance. As this is my last night at Curro's I hope you'll be my guest. Afterwards we can go to El Suizo's perhaps for a farewell glass of *ponche*.'

'When do you leave?' she asked with an icy feeling in her breast.

'Alas, tomorrow. I go to Seville, then to Córdoba.'

'And after that?'

'Who knows? Everything now depends on how successful these dates are.' Carlos looked serious. 'The critics may hate me.'

She laughed. 'I don't know what I should pray for—if they hate you perhaps you'll come back to Granada pretty quickly?'

'Would you want me back as a failure?' he asked lightly.

She paused before answering: 'That's an impossible question. Success seems to be such a part of what you are.'

He grasped her by the hand, his eyes filled for a moment with the light of love. 'With you as my guiding angel, I cannot even contemplate defeat.' He pulled her roughly into his arms. There was nothing brotherly in his kiss. It had all the burning passion of a full-blooded male in it, and Vinny felt again the beginnings of a wild surrender.

'No!' he murmured hoarsely against her cheek. 'We will stay with our good resolutions. It is too soon. You must be sure of me.'

He made her pick up her things from the bed and then he went to the cupboard, unwedged the door and took out a black leather guitar case. 'We'll eat,' he told her. 'They serve fine *tapas* at a place I know near Curro's. Then I must leave you to prepare myself. Will you be all right down town by yourself?'

'I'll go and do some sightseeing,' she told him. 'I haven't seen the Cathedral yet.'

Vinny thanked heaven that the Spanish kept their churches open till the early evening. The thought of wandering around the quarter alone until it was time to go to the club did not appeal to her after her previous experience. She decided to ring Jean anyway and see where she was going to be too. She felt there was another reason for needing to see her friend, but for the moment she could not imagine what it was.

Carlos slid his guitar case with familiar ease on to his shoulder, then treated her to one of his dazzling smiles. Without a word their bodies found each other, but before the stirrings of passion could deflect them from their resolve, Carlos unlocked the door and they went quickly out into the corridor.

The next few hours seemed like a romantic dream to Vinny. They walked slowly, without saying very much to one another, wrapped as lovers often are, in the sweetness of the present moment. It seemed as if the city, waking up from its siesta and donning its evening glitter, had been built expressly as a back drop to their love. On the twin hills north of the town the Moorish palaces were bathed in a rosy glow from the rays of the setting sun, the Generalife, pale and mysterious above its mantling of dark forest, the Alhambra, a deeper hue, spreading magically above the city with its walls and towers. One by one the lights upon the terraced hillside came on, marking out the gentle curve of the avenue which led to the summit.

Down in the town a continuous ribbon of car

lights glittered along the boulevard, and men and women, now freshly groomed, filled the already scented air with the perfume of pomade and musky Arabian oils. They crowded the pavements and swept like an undulating wave into the plazas and pavement cafés, bringing the white-jacketed waiters into renewed life.

Carlos and Vinny mingled unresisting in this slowly moving throng, allowing themselves to go where it carried them, between high white buildings, down narrow cobbled streets, between buildings of ancient stone and, at length, to the plate glass doors of the down town bar Carlos had mentioned.

They stood together at the bar instead of going through into the comedor where whole families were settling down to their evening meal. They stood with limbs intertwined discreetly, elbows resting on the chrome counter, turned towards each other, lips, as they murmured to each other, almost touching. Vinny was powerfully aware of the warmth emanating from his body, the subtle aroma of warm oiled skin, the tang of some hair-dressing which tamed the sleek wild locks of his hair.

'Tell me about South America,' she murmured, picking at the delicious food with as much interest as if it had been thrown together by a third-rate scullion instead of the top-class culinary artist whose pride and joy this little café was. 'Tell me about everything.'

His expression was enigmatic. 'Those years were the years of my apprenticeship,' he told her. 'I was a wild, tough kid in those days, despite my idealism. For a long time I bore a grudge against the man who had turned me into an exile. So it was a time too when I took some hard knocks, not having learned that often nothing is lost by bending with the wind. I took my guitar everywhere with me, on cattle-trains, railroads, mule-trains, travelling across thousands of miles, playing all the time, learning what I could, searching out the best teachers, pushing myself on, sometimes not eating for days on end, other times living like the proverbial king in his palace——' he paused. 'Though of course it was never my palace——' He turned away for a moment. There was an expression on his face which was difficult to fathom, but he turned back, giving her one of his dazzling smiles again. 'So you see, they were good times and bad times.'

'Tell me about the places,' Vinny joked.

This time his face hardened. 'I was very poor, living only from one day to the next, playing in whatever place would take me. Sometimes, in those sort of places, it is easy to acquire patrons, rich people for whom a boy can become their latest toy.' He spoke mockingly. 'I was a good-looking kid.' He turned his gaze full on her, the self-mocking glint in his eyes telling her that he was going to say nothing more. She felt a shutter come down between them, beyond which it seemed at that moment, tactless to want to pry.

'But what about you? I feel so close to you, my angel, it surprises me when I realise how little I really know about you. What are you, just another poor little rich girl?' His lips brushed her temple in a brief possessive kiss.

'I've already told you,' she replied, looking up at him so quickly that her lips brushed his cheek, 'I'm just a teacher of English.'

'My poor little darling, you're not at all my image of a schoolma'am ... and when you get bored with that game? Back into the welcoming bosom of your family, where no doubt you will live on bread and cheese the rest of your days?'

She laughed despite herself. 'You don't believe me, do you?'

'When you have such a fine aristocratic air, no,' he said swiftly, a smile illuminating his face. 'Besides, you are Jean's friend, and her people are not short of a penny or two. Still, enough——' before she could explain how she had come to be a friend of Jean he was ordering another two glasses of *tinto* and the manager, who was also the head waiter and creator of the prepared dishes which gave the café its fame, had come out for a word with El Brasiliano.

'It seems I'm acquiring a name which is worth something,' Carlos told her with not a little amusement after the man had gone. 'Perhaps it will be worth the odd meal now and then, on the house, eh?' He put an arm protectively round her shoulders and when she looked into the mirror on the wall behind the bar she could see his handsome face in profile as he looked down at her, and when he bent his head closer, their hair, his dark, hers light, contrasted strangely, like some allegory of good and evil. Her senses were too benumbed to follow this line of thought far. His very touch seemed to set off fireworks inside her body, and she wondered why the people around them were not dazzled and burnt by the sparks which must surely be flying whenever he embraced her.

It was with a kind of dazed surprise that she realised he was beginning to lift his guitar case on to his shoulders again.

'I must go and prepare,' he told her. 'You go and have a look inside the Cathedral. Go and be appalled by the wedding shrine of Joan the Mad and Philip the Handsome.' He pulled her towards him. 'You are wonderful. It's the luckiest thing that ever happened to me, meeting you.' He kissed her briefly but possessively on the mouth. 'My love, I must ask you to do one favour for me. I seem to have come out without much cash on me. Could you settle this little bill? I'll pay you later when I see you.'

Vinny didn't answer. Carlos was already moving towards the door. 'Mention at the club that you are my guest—they are having to restrict entry these last couple of nights. *Hasta luego!*'

Raising one hand in farewell, he had turned and shouldered his way through the crowd by the door and was gone.

Vinny was overcome by the suddenness of his departure. She felt a sense of shock which made her heart jump into her mouth. She turned back, shaking slightly, to her half-finished glass of wine. In one gulp she had swallowed it. Feeling a little calmer, she gazed thoughtfully at the mirror where but shortly before two images, one dark, one fair, had been reflected. Now there was only her own oval face looking out from the mirror's glassy surface.

Somehow she didn't feel like hanging around the café after this and, the bill paid, she stepped out into the street, suddenly remembering that she had intended to ring Jean. I'll arrange to meet her somewhere before going to the club tonight, she thought, and I ought also to let Mrs Cotton know that I won't be home to dinner. She knew this would not involve much alteration in the arrangements for that evening as it was Luisa's early night and Mrs Cotton had told her that she herself would be cook and it would have to be an easily prepared cold meal, involved as she was on Fridays with the ladies' bridge club.

It was some quarter of an hour before Vinny managed to find a public telephone, and she was annoyed with herself for not seeking out the phone in the café where they had eaten *tapas*.

Mrs Cotton answered in carefully pronounced Spanish and seemed relieved when she could at once break into English.

'I'm sorry, it looks as if I won't be back for dinner——' began Vinny.

'Don't worry about that,' replied Mrs Cotton cheerily. Vinny thought she could hear the murmur of female voices in the background and guessed that the bridge party was still in progress.

'Now are you sure you're all right? You will find a nice place in which to have a good meal?'

'Yes, yes, I'm fine,' replied Vinny. 'I happened to meet a friend,' she went on, wondering wildly if the word conjured up for Mrs Cotton all the vivid pictures which jostled for attention in her own imagination.

'That's nice.'

'May I speak to Jean for a moment?'

'I'm afraid not. She came in, then went out

almost at once. I think she was going to stop off at their usual haunt.'

'You mean El Suizo's?' suggested Vinny.

'That's it. I'd call in there if I were you, dear. Do you know how to get to it?'

As she had been careful to avoid going anywhere near it all that week, she had an extremely clear picture of every road which could possibly lead in its direction. She murmured that she thought she could probably find it, then she let Mrs Cotton get back to her bridge.

It was but a short distance to the café and when she got there she looked eagerly through the windows to see if she could straightaway catch sight of Jean's familiar face. But the place was thronged with people, so she plunged in through the revolving doors to get a better look. It seemed a little early for Jean and Ricky and Co to be there as it was still well before nine, so she wasn't surprised when her perambulation between the little tables drew a blank.

With a slight feeling of disappointment she went outside again and set off without really thinking where she was going. But it was no surprise to find herself at the Cathedral. With an hour or so to spare she could catch up on a little sightseeing, and do Joan the Mad and Philip the Handsome, she thought cheerfully. It seemed that by doing so she would be forging a link between Carlos and herself wherever he was now. She imagined sharing her solitary experience with him in El Suizo's after the performance.

The Cathedral was an enormous edifice of dark Renaissance stone. The hostile gloom of its cavernous interior was offset by the gilded grandiloquence of its specially lit tableaux which came to life out of the dark by the simple method of inserting a five-peseta coin in a slot. Vinny jumped, when, thinking she was lighting only the tableau of Philip the Handsome, the whole dozen or so tableaux in the arcades around the circular outer wall sprang into blazing life.

She had a good look at Philip astride his horse— a proud, fiery, arrogant man in his prime. He seemed to typify all the flashing pride belonging to the macho Spanish male and it seemed as if the sculptor had to embody in this figure everything *los señoritos* held in such esteem. There was a coldness in his look as if there had been nothing else to the man but a life of royal intrigue, making him calculating and aloof. As for Joan—was she mad for love of this man? wondered Vinny. Or made mad by loving him? Or maddened by his untouchable air of calculating hauteur? What had there been of softness and trust in their relationship? What of love? Yet their match had been famed throughout the civilised world, an embodiment of high feeling to which ordinary mortals could not hope to aspire.

She left the Cathedral rather sooner than she had expected. She felt strangely disturbed by the emotions it had aroused and she walked aimlessly for a while among the still busy streets as if to shake off some infection. At length she turned her steps in the direction of El Suizo's again, and, ready for a cup of coffee, resolved to find herself a table this time and stay until it was time to go on to Curro's.

In no time she found herself being revolved briskly into the animated scene behind the plate-glass windows. She was bemusedly searching for an empty seat when she heard voices calling her name. Looking up, she was relieved to see Ricky and Paco waving to her from one of the booths along the wall. She went to join them, asking at once where Jean had got to.

Ricky looked sullenly down at the table in front of him without speaking, but Paco laughed and said, 'She's busy all week. With amour.' He burst out laughing again and cuffed Ricky playfully on the shoulder. 'He is in a black humour, taking affairs of the heart so seriously. I tell him he is mad, but he doesn't listen. Come and help me get some sense into him.'

Vinny sat down on the chair Paco adroitly pulled up from another table.

'It's not worth the candle, is it?' he asked her when they were all settled. 'You tell him. He ignores my fatherly advice.'

The young Spaniard cockled back on his chair in high good spirits and a passing waiter growled 'Hey, *majo*, watch out!' as he skirted him, tray held dangerously high on one hand above his head.

Ricky raised his eyes to Vinny's. 'This clown is beginning to get on my nerves. She can do what she likes. I'm just a bit tired, that's all. I've had a busy week with exams.'

'Not too busy to be every night at Curro's,' teased Paco, taking out tobacco and cigarette papers. He turned his attention to Vinny. 'You have missed something this week,' he told her.

'I know,' she replied. 'I intend to make up for it tonight.'

'Good. We go that way too. And pretty soon, so as to get in.' He stopped abruptly. 'It's strictly limited entry.' Then he shrugged. 'You are a gorgeous blonde. No man is going to say "no" to you. You'll get in all right.'

'As a matter of fact I happened to bump into El Brasiliano earlier this evening,' she told him, trying to keep her tone casual. 'He told me to tell them on the door that I would be his guest tonight.'

Paco looked at her without speaking for a minute, his dark eyes blank. Then he turned abruptly to Ricky.

'Another *café solo, amigo mio*?' he asked. Turning back to Vinny, 'You too?' he asked. 'I'm feeling generous tonight.'

Vinny didn't have time to examine the peculiar reaction which Paco's sudden change in manner had aroused in her, for at that moment a crowd of Paco's friends arrived and there was a general reorganisation of furniture which involved several rather long and apparently dramatic interchanges with the people sitting nearby whose tables were swiftly being stripped of their accompanying chairs. Paco became central to all this, and when the seating arrangements were finally settled, Vinny found she was wedged between Ricky and a tall Spaniard with a Zapata moustache.

'She teaches English. Now's your chance Joaquin!' called Paco across the table, and for the next hour, until they decided to move on to Curro's, Joaquin practised his not too fluent English on Vinny.

She noticed that Ricky was silent throughout all

this and sipped his coffee with scarcely more than an odd word to add to the banter flowing around him.

CHAPTER TEN

THE atmosphere was electric as they walked into the club, and despite the rule of limited entrance, the place was already packed, with extra seating being brought in and people standing on benches at the back.

When Vinny had told the man at the door that she was El Brasiliano's guest he had asked her name and on consulting a piece of card which he drew from out of his top pocket had waved her through, calling out to a passing waiter to show them to a reserved table as he did so.

Paco had been mildly impressed, but Vinny had looked round for Jean as soon as they were seated. 'Did she say she would be here?' she asked Paco, but he shrugged noncommittally.

'She will turn up. Late, no doubt.'

Vinny was impatient. She had remembered now why it had seemed important to speak to her friend, and she couldn't help casting frequent glances towards the crowd around the door. However, the compère was already shouting for people to stand back, and through the opening that the crowd made Vinny caught a glimpse of the glossy piled hair of the dancers and a guitar raised above a player's head as they shouldered their way through the cheering crowd. In a moment her eyes were dwelling on the bronzed features of the man with whom she had so recently shared such intimacy. Now his eyes swept coolly over the audience and his easy relaxed smile acknowledged their cheers.

Miraculously with the first chord the crowd fell silent, and it was in an almost religious hush that they drank in the music that followed.

Carlos was undoubtedly the star of the group now, the man they had all come to hear. This time he sang more, taking the centre of the stage where the first time she had heard him he had been content to remain in the shadows at the back. It was with such ease that he seemed to take control of the audience that Vinny could only marvel at this presence and authority. It was as if he was alive to every nuance in the crowd's collective mood, for he would caress them into a state of swooning delight, then little by little lead them on to a state of wild ecstasy, taking such breathtaking technical risks with his voice, as Vinny, a singer herself, knew, that she could scarcely stop herself from crying out at his daring.

There was something primitive in the quality of his voice, something savage which was at variance with the cool, rather detached and cultivated manner in which he spoke to her in English. She had had a hint of this untamed force in their brief moments of lovemaking when no words had been uttered, but even so, it made her realise that there was much about him that was still hidden from her. Much, she thought, with a tremor, even on the more accessible levels of their relationship which was hidden from her, especially answers to such questions as: had he been telling the truth about Jean when he denied having seen her during the week?

There was still no sign of her redheaded friend, and she licked her lips in sudden apprehension. There were many other questions too—questions about Carlos's private life, his—she shied away from the thought, but it hammered till she framed the words—questions about his other 'loves', his other 'relationships', that she longed to have answered. She didn't doubt, couldn't doubt now, after witnessing the adulation bestowed on him tonight that there were other, many other relationships of, at least on the one side, a very passionate nature. Insecurity fanned the seed of jealousy.

With all this adoration coming to him, why should he want her? Was it true, as she had angrily suggested that afternoon, that he wanted her to be in that dreadful phrase she had used, his 'Granada stop-over'? She felt her muscles tense. It was no effort to forget such nagging doubts at this minute under the spell of his music, but whenever his rakish smile flashed an invitation to the crowd she felt a sick panic at the thought that his smile with all its promise was not for her alone.

In the midst of the tumult that burst out as the last note died, Vinny felt a tap on her shoulder and turned to find herself looking up into the mischievously smiling face of Jean. She indicated to Vinny to budge up and they squashed together on the same chair. Vinny wanted an answer to her question at once, but she just had time to ask: 'Where have you been?' when the next piece—a Malagueña—was announced. 'Backstage, of course, but I'll tell you later.' Jean was grinning with a barely contained excitement. 'Isn't it wonderful?' She looked round at the thronging crowd who once again were as silent as a church congregation.

At the end of the next piece, as the applause burst around them, Jean whispered in Vinny's ear: 'I haven't seen you all week. Everything been O.K.?'

'Fine, thanks,' replied Vinny. 'But what have you been up to?'

'I've been with him,' answered Jean, nodding towards the stage. 'Is Ricky still absolutely furious with me?'

Vinny shrugged, a sickening lurch in her stomach, telling her just how hard Jean's news had struck her. 'Ask him yourself,' she said offhandedly. 'I'm sure you'll be able to talk him round.' She turned her head deliberately towards the stage just as Carlos came forward holding his guitar by his side, his eyes moving lazily over the crowd. So he had been lying to her. She felt sick. He had told her he had not seen Jean after that first night, but he had lied to her. Just then his eye searched her out and for an instant their glances locked. He gave a strange sweet, almost secret smile and her blood froze as if she had been suddenly stripped naked. Everyone could surely see what had passed between them. But no one's head turned, nothing changed, and he had already swung his guitar into the playing position and was allowing his fingers to span the strings idly as he introduced the next song.

'Has anything happened?' whispered Jean in the

hush before the first notes sounded. Vinny shook
her head, giving, she hoped, a passable imitation
of someone paying close attention to the piece
about to be performed. It was a dramatic song,
with hard-driving rhythms, which Carlos carried in
a torrent of rich, heavy chords—but it was about a
woman, married, who had gone to the river with
her lover, and told how he felt when he discovered
she wore a wedding ring. Carlos played with such
passion that the perspiration trickled down his
forehead, and when he finished to an ecstasy of
cheering his hair was tousled and lay in damp locks
over his forehead.

One of the dancers, the older one, took off one
of her scarves and wiped his brow, and the crowd
went mad with approval in their appreciation of
the significance of such an action.

'If they only knew,' grinned Jean, apparently
forgetting the huffiness of Vinny's earlier response.
'She's married to the *tocador* of the group and he
never lets her out of his sight for a minute.'

'Where there's a will there's a way,' answered
Vinny tartly as Carlos, touching the scarf gallantly
to his lips for a moment handed it back to the
woman with his familiar rakish smile.

Vinny felt she could bear it no longer, but looking desperately round for a way out, she realised
that she could only draw unwelcome attention to
herself if she tried to fight her way outside now.
Besides, she thought, suddenly grim, she would
enjoy having it out with him. She would let him
know in no uncertain terms exactly what she
thought about his philandering.

She sat back in her chair as best she could with

Jean bobbing up and down excitedly beside her and resolved to remain totally unmoved for the rest of the show.

Jean's crowd, including the still morose Ricky, hung about after the performers retired to their dressing-room, and let the rest of the audience get out before themselves, rising to their feet and going towards the stairs. Several people were waiting outside the door which Vinny remembered led on to the passage where the changing room was and Jean, cheerily pushing her way through, was already telling Paco and Ricky that they were going to have the privilege of being allowed into the backstage area, so long as they both kept in her good books, when the manager came out and held up his arms. '*Perdone,*' he said, and a rapid flow of Spanish followed which at once brought a frown to Jean's face.

'Oh well, that's that for the time being,' she said when the man stopped talking. 'We can either go on somewhere else leaving a message to say where we've gone, or we can sit here till they come out, and drink some of this dreadful, overpriced *tinto*. Which is it to be, gang?'

'Go somewhere else,' said Ricky at once.

'O.K.' Jean was amiable.

'*Que pasa, que pasa?*' asked Paco, coming out of the gents to rejoin them.

'You know the Press were here in full force tonight,' said Jean, turning to him, 'apparently the group are giving interviews or something. They'll be some time yet.'

'Let's go,' repeated Ricky. 'I don't fancy hanging around here.'

The rest of the group agreed and Vinny had no choice but to follow. Jean was just about to tell the manager the name of the bar they had decided on when a woman who seemed to Vinny vaguely familiar appeared at the door of the dressing-room. As she came out on to the stairs Carlos appeared behind her and, without looking either to left or right, followed the woman through the bar towards the street.

Vinny watched them pass by as if turned to ice, for she suddenly remembered where she had seen the woman. It was the one from the tower, the one who had seemed to have such a startling effect on Carlos, making him rush off in such haste. She was still wearing the large dark glasses, but this time had on a brief black diamanté-covered evening dress and instead of the gold hoop ear-rings she wore something small and glittery and expensive-looking dangling from her ears to match the several bangles on her wrists. She was swinging a bunch of car keys from one elegantly manicured hand as she turned to Carlos with a smile that was wholly as dazzling as his own.

'*Caro*, here! Take them!'

Vinny's Spanish was good enough to translate her words.

Without more ado the woman went out through the door with Carlos closely following.

'Press!' exploded Jean in disbelief. 'A likely story!' She turned to the manager and said something to him and he began to spread his arms.

'Well,' she said, 'apparently the Press *are* there. They've already taken a few photos. But who she was he doesn't seem to know. I guess we've lost El

Brasiliano for the night. Come on, kids, *vamonos!'*

Vinny was shocked at Jean's sudden recovery. She envied the younger girl's ability to take life so lightly. She doubted whether the pain she felt inside would ever permit her to switch so flippantly into another mood like that.

Worse, however, was to come. When they all got outside the alley was blocked by an enormous white sports car and Carlos was standing holding the keys, looking down at the car as if trying to judge whether he could back it out along the narrow alley without damaging its expensive paintwork. The woman must have said something, for suddenly they moved into each other's arms and for a moment stood like that without speaking, as Jean, Ricky, Paco and finally Vinny squeezed through the narrow gap between the car and the building. Carlos didn't even notice them, for when Vinny turned at the corner of the street he was still looking down into the eyes of the woman he held in his arms.

The weekend passed in a blur. Vinny felt physically sick and was unable to hide her state of mind from anyone. Mrs Cotton surmised that she was due for a bout of Spanish tummy and insisted that she spend the rest of the time in bed. Guiltily Vinny put up a mild protest, claiming that she was really quite all right, just overtired, but when she burst into tears Mrs Cotton would brook no opposition and the girl was bundled upstairs and kept supplied with a regular flow of medicinal drinks throughout the day.

When Jean came into sit by her bed late in the

afternoon, one look at the wan face and feverishly bright eyes told her that one dinner guest at least would be absent from that evening's get-together.

'And probably Ricky will give me the cold shoulder,' she fretted, wandering round the room like a caged animal. 'I know I've been rotten to him this week, but it's not as if there's any understanding between us yet.'

Vinny raised her cool face from the pillow for a moment. 'There was no understanding with Denny, either, I suppose,' she said tartly.

Jean sighed and then lifted her chin. There was the flicker of her old mischievous smile again. 'Why do men want to tie us down so?' she demanded spiritedly. 'They want *us* to commit ourselves singlemindedly to them, but how many of them will show us the same fidelity? It's too one-sided. I want a piece of the action too.'

Vinny couldn't help halfheartedly agreeing. 'But,' she added, 'surely if you find the right person, there'd be no room for anyone else?'

'Maybe,' agreed Jean reluctantly. 'It's finding the right one, though, isn't it? And I'm afraid most men are in the Carlos mould, though less ostentatiously successful. I feel like taking a leaf out of his book myself. Love them and leave them—that's my motto.'

Yet after the dinner party that evening Jean said no more along these lines and Vinny, spending Sunday in bed too, heard the sound of Ricky's car in the drive as he called to pick her up for a day in the mountains. The dinner party must have been a success from Mrs Cotton's point of view too, for in the following days it became a familiar sight to see his car in the drive whenever she returned from work.

She went to her classes each day with a strange sense of unreality pervading everything as if it was all taking place at one remove and she was merely a puppet going through the motions of some already scripted scenario.

A card had arrived on the Wednesday. She saw it in the post box on the gate at the end of the drive on her way to work, and took it out with shaking hands. It said: 'Sorry I missed you at Curro's. What happened? Tour seems to be going well. *Hasta la vista*. Carlos.'

Vinny held it for a good two minutes between fingers which trembled uncontrollably, before putting it deep into the inner pocket of her bag. It was with a sense of detachment, despite the stinging tears that sprang to her eyes, that she made her way down the lane to the bus stop.

What had she expected? More false declarations of love? More lies? At least the message was short and to the point. She bunched her fists. Perhaps, in his arrogance, Carlos thought that that was all she needed to keep her waiting faithfully for his return. She made a resolution on the way to work, and it was a changed girl who stepped down in the Plaza Neuva.

'Oh, come on, Jean! Don't be a dead legs!' chided Vinny some weeks later. 'It'll be enormous fun, and who cares whether Ricky will be there or not. All the gang are keen and it looks as if there'll be three

car-loads so far, if you come. You can't let everybody down.'

Jean looked up from her book. Ricky had had
to go and spend a ten-day holiday in Germany with
his people and, amazingly, Jean had made it the
opportunity to catch up on, as she claimed, some
much neglected reading.

'You don't *have* to choose *War and Peace*, do you?'
scoffed Vinny. 'It'll take more than ten days.'

'I shan't necessarily stop just because he comes
back,' retorted Jean. 'If the last few weeks are anything to go by he won't give you chance to read
even half a paragraph,' laughed Vinny. She teasingly flicked the book shut. 'Come with us. You
can read all the way in the car if you let me drive.'

Jean looked up with a grin. 'Oh hell, if you're
going to twist my arm, why not! I can send him
postcards, and his letters aren't such literary mas-
terpieces that it's worth missing out on a few days'
break for them.' She jumped up. 'You win. Tell me
all about it. Where are you taking me?'

It was a few days later when the three cars set off.
There was an old Citroën, driven by Paco and
carrying three Spanish friends from his year at
university, a Packard driven by Ricky's room-mate
with a couple of other Americans and Joaquin, so
he could practise his English, and finally Jean and
Vinny in the little English two-seater.

They were heading north and had decided to
drive as far as Toledo in one of those spontaneous
group decisions which had followed on Vinny's
somewhat wistful comment one evening in El
Suizo's that, despite her brief stay in Madrid when

she first arrived, she had been unable to find the time to visit what was often described as the real capital of Spain.

'Never seen Toledo!' exclaimed Paco. 'But you must. If you go nowhere else, you must go there.'

'Let's take her up next week!' suggested Toni, one of the Spaniards, and an American said: 'Count me in if there's any sightseeing in the offing. I've been in one goddamned town too long.'

'Getting the wanderlust again, honey?' asked his girl-friend, and when the growls of warning had died down from the rest of the gang, Paco had said: 'I move that a decision on a possible Toledo trip be made as soon as possible.'

'You can tell he's studying business management,' scoffed Anna. 'But count me in too.'

It was quickly agreed that with the consent of the absent Jean they would take three cars between them and, driving through the night, would head straight for Toledo itself. 'No messing,' said Paco.

'As long as we don't plan to stay in five-star hotels,' said Joaquín, 'count me in too. My purse does not stretch at this time so deep.'

'His English is really coming on,' mocked Paco. 'He must be having private tuition!' He made a show of looking pointedly at Vinny, but she refused to be teased.

'Let's be serious,' she said. 'When are we leaving?'

They were now in the middle of the olive-growing area. After an evening start it was nightfall by the time they found themselves driving along with olive groves stretching around them on all sides in eerily geometric formations to the far horizon.

There were few villages of any size on the route and the white-walled *fincas* which glimmered eerily out of the dark were without exception devoid of any sign of life.

'Early to bed, early to rise.,' commented Jean at one stage, and she had switched on the car radio to some French all-night music programme. The light on the dashboard glowed comfortably and Vinny, preparing to take over the driving in the early hours, settled down to have a nap. Despite the steady purring of the engine and the warmth inside the little car, however, she found it difficult to get any rest. Her dreams were haunted by the emptiness of the apparently fun-filled last few weeks. She had made a superhuman effort to get out and enjoy herself and had flirted outrageously with the boys in El Suizo's, while making sure she didn't give the impression that she was after any serious involvement with any of them. The rather lugubrious Joaquin had seemed particularly smitten, but she had managed quite successfully to keep him at arm's length by spreading her attentions impartially among them all. It had been fun, in its way. There was something satisfying about the informal way they all met down in the clubs and cafés of the old town, but in her heart Vinny knew it was all a sham. Only in the privacy of her own room did she allow her true feelings to come to the surface, and many was the night she had cried herself to sleep at the remembrance of those flashing dark eyes and the sombre good looks of the absent Carlos.

It was not as if he failed to keep in touch. He sent postcards from Seville, from Cordoba, and from Madrid, and from several places in between. None of them had had any forwarding address and there were only brief scribbled messages: 'I think they like us—the tour goes on. . . .' 'Greetings from Galicia', 'Next stop Castile. . . .' Each was as brief as the next but each bore the familiar ending *'hasta la vista'*—till we meet again. By now Vinny was able to read these words with what she thought was a cynical smile and it did something to still the flicker of hope that sometimes in idle moments disturbed her equilibrium.

Stretching her legs as much as she could in the confined space of the passenger seat, she gazed out at the strange shapes the olive trees made. They looked like an army of little gnarled dwarfs marching resolutely across the hillside, but she couldn't make up her mind whether they were spirits of good or evil.

'Penny for them,' said Jean eventually.

Vinny looked at her friend. Jean had caught her in the middle of a reverie about him, of course. Truthfully she answered, 'I don't know how you could have forgotten him so easily.' There was no criticism in her tone, just surprise and wonder.

'Who? Denny?' asked Jean unexpectedly.

'No,' corrected Vinny with a half smile, 'I mean Carlos. Who else?'

'Who said I'd forgotten *him*?' replied Jean with a laugh. 'He was gorgeous. I only wish I could have got to know him better. Still, that week did bear fruit,' she chuckled. 'Don't be taken in by Ricky's quiet manner, like I was at first. He's all male.'

'I'm sure he is,' murmured Vinny, but her

thoughts were already flirting with the way Carlos had smiled at her in his hotel room, the way he had held her, the way the hunger of his body had excited a similar need in hers. She stifled a sigh of exasperation with herself. Had she forgotten that he had talked her into eating *tapas* with him afterwards and having eaten to his satisfaction had turned round and asked her to foot the bill? She clenched her fists. That sort of action spoke eloquently of the sort of man he was and what he thought of her, far more than any brief expression of physical hunger in a scruffy hotel room or a collection of pretty picture postcards designed to keep her sweet for his eventual return.

'Let me drive,' she asked suddenly. At least it would give her something else to think about and perhaps break the train of her idiotic and soul-destroying obsession.

CHAPTER ELEVEN

IT was dawn as they approached the valley of the Tagus over which, on a high crag like a castle in a fairytale, rose the spires and towers of the walled city which had once been the royal seat of the Spanish kings.

'Toledo!' breathed Jean. 'Embattled fortress, city of romance!' She grinned. 'What fun to be tourists. We must do the El Grecos first, and the Mosque and the Alcazar, and eat lots of marzipan all the time and——'

'Steady on!' laughed Vinny, changing down as

she drove the car up the steeply cobbled road which led into the city through the southern gates.

Paco was in the car in front and she was second in the convoy. Jean turned round to give the car following the thumbs-up sign, and as she did so something on the side of the road made Vinny's blood freeze.

She missed her gear change and the car juddered. 'Jean,' she cried, 'did you see that poster?'

Jean turned back. 'What was it?'

Vinny gulped. 'It looked like a photo of Carlos.'

'Hey, really? Where?' Jean was agog.

'Is it likely?' asked Vinny doubtfully.

'He's probably been playing up here,' Jean informed her. 'Didn't he say he'd be on tour for a while?'

Vinny had been unable to show Jean the postcards she had received, and as she always left the house first it had been an easy matter to go through the post herself first. 'Are we still in Castile?' asked Vinny.

'Sure. It's a big place and this is still it. Why?'

'It's just that he mentioned something about a Castilian tour,' she said vaguely.

'It'll be him, then,' replied Jean. 'He's all the rage now, according to the music critic of the *Madrileño*.' She paused. 'I can't understand why you're not more interested. It's really exciting that we actually met him when he was unknown and knew even then that he was going to be something really big.'

Vinny drove carefully up the steep hill and through the gates of the city.

'He was interested in you, you know,' said Jean

unexpectedly. 'That night when you didn't come back with me he seemed really put out.'

Vinny wanted to confide in Jean, but there seemed no way to frame the words.

'Hey, stop a minute. Can you stop on a one in three?' Jean flagged down the car behind and leant across to give a couple of toots on the car horn to the group in front. Both cars pulled into the side of the road. Jean jumped out and walked back a few yards. She beckoned excitedly to Vinny and with a sense of foreboding Vinny climbed out of the car and made her way back to where Jean was excitedly jigging up and down.

'He's beautiful, isn't he?' She squeezed Vinny's arm. 'Look, everybody! Look who's in town tonight!'

The rest of the gang crowded round.

'At the Hotel Royal too,' observed Paco. 'Do you think they will allow us in there?' He looked round at the travel-stained group.

'He's certainly playing the high spots,' said Jean. 'What do you say we go and get tickets first off?'

There was a chorus of agreement to which Vinny thought it not worth adding a note of dissension. She could always plead a headache and stay in her hotel room with a good book and a slab of the marzipan for which Toledo was famed. On the other hand, she thought, as they all piled back into the cars, it might be quite amusing to see the expression on Carlos's face as she swanned into the hotel with a bunch of men friends as escort. That would put paid to his vision of her playing the part of my lady of the tears in Granada!

It was with the renewed energy which comes from a sense of wrongs about to be righted that she checked in with the others at the two-star Hotel Landazuri.

There were photos that evening in the local paper. Photos of Carlos being received by a local dignitary. Photos of Carlos opening a new swimming pool.

'She's still around, then,' observed Jean, pointing to the figure of a woman in dark glasses whose face smiled up at Carlos as he shook hands with some local bigwig.

They had, even to Vinny's disappointment, been unable to obtain tickets for the performance. It had been sold out within a day of the posters going up, they were told. Evidently news of his genius had travelled fast, and Jean, despite her disappointment, went round preening herself somewhat for having been the first of the group to draw attention to him back in the Curro's days.

Vinny didn't know whether she was pleased or not at being denied a confrontation. One thing was certain, whenever she saw his handsome face smiling sombrely out of the posters which blanketed the town, she felt the sick weight of longing in the pit of her stomach.

Despite the beauty of Toledo, she longed to escape.

She was beginning to find the sombre little alleys honeycombing the oldest part of the town both oppressive and ominous. 'There's something evil about this place,' she said as they made their way back to the hotel to change for dinner. 'I hate it here. It's really spooky.'

'Don't you find all medieval cities a little weird?' asked Toni. 'When you imagine what used to go on it's not surprising.'

The thought seemed to make them all strangely subdued and, with the fact that the disco bar they went to later on was almost empty because everyone was at the El Brasiliano concert, their first night was not the success they'd envisaged.

The following day was spent in regular sightseeing. Vinny felt that there was something savagely appropriate in the El Greco's for which the town was also famed. She felt that the violent sinuosity of lines and the dramatic hues in which he painted seemed to match so closely something of the turbulence of her own thoughts that it was with surprise that she realised she could not actually summon up, with the strength of these feelings, the figure of the man on whom her thoughts were fixed.

She left the chapel where the great painting of the Death of Count Orgaz was housed with an urge to shake off the oppression she felt with this continual preoccupation with death and salvation, but everywhere she turned in the narrow streets were shops selling finely wrought swords of Toledo steel. There were foils and sabres and every kind of medieval instrument of torture which the suppliers to the tourists trade deemed saleable, and it was in desperation that she sought an escape from the sight of things which seemed to mock the sorrow that pierced her own heart like a fine-edged sword.

While the rest of the group, spirits now restored, were fooling about in one of the squares with the swords they had inevitably purchased she decided to go and seek a quiet refuge in the church of Santa Maria la Blanca.

'Not another church!' cried Toni. 'You're a glutton for punishment, Vinny.'

She smiled. 'I just feel like a walk by myself, actually.'

No one seemed to want to drag themselves along and they arranged to meet later at a café they had found that had an American jukebox and a cheap but rather fine seafood bar. It was with something like a flicker of relief that Vinny set off alone towards the ancient church in the Jewish quarter.

Santa Maria la Blanca was an unpretentious building, once a mosque, later a synagogue, and even later a farm store. Now restored to its original simplicity, it was a fine example of Almohade style with its column after column of white horseshoe arches and decorated capitals.

It seemed an appropriate setting in which to nurse her grief, but so lost did she become in the serenity of its cool white columns that little by little a tranquil joy began to soothe her spirits. She sat alone on the shallow steps in front of the simple altar for a long time after the last visitor had left, and it was only when she stood up to go that she became aware of a dark shadow motionless under one of the farthest arches. As she made her way slowly towards the great oak door, the shadow detached itself from its place and began to move towards her. There was an eagerness in its step and when she turned fully in that direction, there came a cry of surprise and recognition.

'*Cariña*, is this real?'

She froze. Like the black knight in an ancient

legend, Carlos was outlined against the stark simplicity of the whitewashed columns of Santa Maria la
Blanca.

'No!' Her voice was a croak of astonishment.

He came slowly towards her, his face strained,
she noticed, from too many nights on the road,
but suffused with a look of such plausible love and
tenderness Vinny was momentarily bowled over by
it. Her thoughts flying, she stood her ground until
he was a pace or two in front of her.

Then: 'No lady-friend?' she asked coolly.

He grinned rakishly. 'Even I have to be alone
some time,' he replied.

Anger, and hurt humiliation, rose up inside her.
She could think of no words which could adequately
express her pain. She turned blindly towards the exit.

'*Cara*, wait! Where are you going to in such a
hurry?'

When she failed to reply he sprang to bar her
escape with a few athletic strides. His smile had
gone now and a frown shadowed his face.

'My love, my sweet love, whatever is the matter?'
He made as if to take her in his arms, but she
stepped out of his reach with an angry swish of her
hair.

'What has happened? How is it you are here of
all places? Were you looking for me?'

His face expressed bewilderment which would at
any other time have disarmed her. Now she simply
glowered, unable to contain her anger.

'Am I looking for you?' she said at last in a low
voice full of scorn. 'The now famous El
Brasiliano——' she uttered his stage name with
an unmistakable note of derision in it—'his

pride is so great he thinks that every woman he meets must become a victim of his perfidious charms!'

Carlos's face wore a mask of utter astonishment. 'Is this Lavinia?' he asked, half aloud.

She drew herself up, long blonde hair gleaming like an aura in the rays of the setting sun which came in through the windows of the chapel. 'This is a Lavinia who has unfortunately seen through you. Another Granadine lover will have to be found. Though no doubt that will be an easy task for the hero of the moment.'

'But I don't want anybody but you,' he said dully, like a child repeating the lines of a poem. He stood looking at her for a moment, his face suddenly dead as if all the light had been drawn from it. 'I don't want anybody but you,' he repeated at last.

Vinny was about to push past him to the door when there came the first approaching sound of many voices raised in excited anticipation.

Carlos turned with a cry of exasperation. '*Dios*, will they never leave me in peace!' He took hold of Vinny by the arm before she knew what was happening and dragged her back under the next row of arches so that they were partly hidden behind one of the columns.

'Listen to me,' he said with a sign of his old authority. 'I don't know what has happened since we last met, but I'm sure it can all be explained. There's no time now. If I'm not mistaken it's the Press out there again, come to give me a royal send-off. I'm due in Madrid tonight. But look——' He fumbled in his pocket for a piece of card. 'Contact

me here. Such a lot has happened, it would take
too long to explain. But please believe me, my darling, my feelings for you are not as ephemeral as
you seem to think.'

He had no sooner managed to get these words
out when the great double doors were flung back
and a group of people burst into the chapel. For a
moment they seemed stunned by the silent beauty
of the place, but though Carlos held Vinny
motionless in his arms for a moment they were at
once observed as the group advanced under the
first row of arches.

'Run now,' he told her. 'Don't let them stop you
or you'll have no privacy.'

Her thoughts in a whirl, she had no choice but
to do as he said, and as she flitted from the building
she could hear the pop of flash bulbs as the
Pressmen got to work.

'My God, what's happened to you?' Jean's out-
spoken astonishment turned all eyes on Vinny as
she came into the bar and tried to find a seat without being noticed. The last thing she wanted was
to be the centre of a lot of prying questions, but
the directness of Jean's query was the straw that
unblocked the dam. Appalled at herself, Vinny
found that she was suddenly leaning on the bar
sobbing like a baby. Jean put an arm protectively
around her, then turned angry eyes on the rest of
the gang. 'Look here, you lot, this is between Vinny
and me, now just buzz off somewhere and play
soldiers for a while—O.K.?'

'I'll sort them out,' said Anna briskly. 'Come on,
lads! *Vamonos! Pronto!*'

With a few shrugs and sidelong glances they allowed the American girl to herd them outside.

'Now then,' said Jean after ordering Vinny a cognac, 'spill the beans to your Aunty Jean.'

'You can't be my aunt at your age,' said Vinny between snuffles.

'I'm only a year younger than you, for heaven's sake,' snapped Jean in mock anger. She took Vinny's hand and patted it. 'Is it anything you can talk about?'

Vinny blew her nose and pushed her sticky hair out of her eyes.

'I feel such a fool,' she began. 'I thought I had my feelings under control.' She looked at Jean through watery eyes. 'It's Carlos—I've just seen him.'

'Carlos?' Jean at once looked alert. 'Did you speak to him?'

'Yes.'

Jean sat back. 'I've always had the feeling there was something happening there,' she said slowly. 'Tell me about it.'

As best she could in her confused state Vinny told Jean the outlines of what had happened.

'So why the tears?' demanded Jean. 'What more do you want? He's a gorgeous man.'

'Yes, but don't you see?' cut in Vinny in exasperation at her friend's slowness. 'He said he hadn't seen you that week when he was at Curro's. He said to check with you if I didn't believe him—presumably thinking I wouldn't bother. What's so rotten is that if he was lying then how could I ever trust him to tell the truth about anything? And it was you yourself who called him a gigolo—he knows my people are rolling in money and then I had to pay for the tapas, and then there's that glamorous older woman following him around. He practically told me that when he was in South America he was a—oh, what's the word——'

'Forget South America for a minute!' said Jean. 'What's all this about me? What did you check with me?'

'Whether you'd been with him all those times when you came in at dawn—that week when you kept leaving those cards about melting glaciers——'

Jean was laughing by this time so much that tears were running down her cheeks too. 'You are a clot of the first water,' she said at last when her laughter had subsided. 'Of course I was out all night. I was with Ricky. I made him go to every one of those damned performances. I admit it was Carlos I was wild about to begin with, that's why Ricky was so narked, poor love. But I never got to see Carlos by himself, even. He used to slope off back to the hotel by himself straight afterwards, too whacked, I should think, to do anything but collapse in his little truckle bed and go straight to sleep. He just puts so much energy into his playing he'd have to be superhuman to have the stamina to do much else!' She chuckled. 'And you thought I was with him? I should be so lucky! No, it was the rest of the group I used to meet. Especially Ribero. We used to just drink and yarn and they'd play a bit, and we'd just have a good time.' She sighed. 'The stuff we write when we're in love! That melting glacier was me, melting for Ricky. I guess I am a one-man woman after all.'

She took hold of Vinny's hand and held it
tightly. 'You are a fool! I'm sure all the other things
can be explained too. If it was just money he was
after he's in the money himself now. Go and see
him when you get back, 'At least go and listen to
what he has to say.'

Vinny dried her eyes. It was as if a flicker of
light had appeared at the end of a long dark street.
She took the card he had given her from out of her
bag.

'Marqués de Altolaguirre Benevente——' she
read, then there was the address of a bank in
Madrid.

'Strange,' said Jean. 'It must be a forwarding
address. Never mind, just do as he says. We'll be
going through Madrid tomorrow. No reason why
we can't stop off for an hour or so. I'll prime the
gang.'

Vinny could only sit there, turning the piece of
card over and over in her hand. The Marqués de
Altolaguirre Benevente, whoever he was, would
perhaps lead her to the arms of the man who had
once told her that fate had brought them together.

The girl on the reception desk took the card Vinny
showed her and pressed a buzzer on the switch-
board in front of her. In Spanish she said:
'Someone to see El Marqués....*Cómo se llama?*'
she leaned forward to Vinny. 'Name?'

Vinny told her in a voice made small with awe
at the grandeur of the place in which she now found
herself. It was apparently the H.Q. of one of the
many privately owned banks whose spectacular
steel and glass tower blocks lined the main boule-

vard of Granada, and here in the capital were similarly overwhelming in their opulent modernity.

'Go up. Twenty-second floor.' The girl spoke briskly in English and before Vinny could ask her any further questions she had turned to the next person.

Vinny walked selfconsciously across the cream marble floor of the foyer which was as vast as a dance floor, and stood in confusion before the line of ten lifts until a set of doors opened silently in front of her. Curiosity getting the better of her nervousness, she stepped into the carpeted interior. Inside it was all mirrors and she took a quick peep at herself behind the lift boy's back. Whoever this Marqués was, haughty Spanish grandee, or whatever, she must look her best. With hardly any sense of motion the lift came to a stop and the lift boy stepped to one side so that Vinny could alight.

She found herself in what must be the top of the building as there was a large glass-domed roof. But before she had time to take in the fountain and the two fully grown palm trees and the amazing sight of real birds fluttering among the branches of the other small trees in full flower, her attention was claimed by the tall figure of Carlos himself walking towards her with arms outstretched in greeting.

He was wearing his usual black, but there was a subtle difference in the quality of the silk shirt he wore and the fine cloth of his tight black trousers.

For a moment he held her in his arms without speaking, then kissing her lingeringly on the temple he looked at last into her eyes.

'You're here, my darling. That makes me feel that half the battle is won. Come. I am unfortunately in the middle of a somewhat heated discussion, but I think you should know what is going on.'

He led her by the hand to a beige velvet-covered door and pushed it open.

In the spacious room beyond she saw a number of people. Her glance at once picked out the woman in the dark glasses who had appeared so frequently of late by Carlos's side. She saw also the two dancers she had first seen at Curro's and the man she took to be the manager of the group. The amiable-looking guitarist whom Jean had told her was called Ribero was also there. A couple of men in business suits, one of them arranging papers on one of the large desks by the window, completed the gathering.

Everyone looked up as Carlos came back into the room as if they had been waiting for him before going on with their discussion.

One of the men by the desk at once addressed Carlos in a stream of Spanish. Carlos held up his hand. 'Please, I must introduce Lavinia Steele. I would appreciate it too if you would speak in English.'

The man Ribero said something in Spanish which sounded unprintable, but he gave a little mock bow to Lavinia and held his hand apologetically to his heart.

'He says that counts him out,' grinned Carlos.

The man said something else and Carlos laughed. 'He thinks it is a clever move on my part to defeat the opposition. Now come and meet my sister Elena.'

The woman in the dark glasses came forward to

take hold of both Lavinia's hands in hers, then she hugged her impulsively. 'At last—I've been so looking forward to meeting you, my dear,' she said in her attractive accent.

Vinny felt her heart lift—not only at her warm reception but at the explanation for the woman's relationship with Carlos. Relief swamped over her, bringing little tears to the corners of her eyes.

Carlos looked sharply at her but went on with the introductions. Vinny was too overcome to take much notice. She gathered merely that the two men were something to do with the Bank.

'And the Marqués?' she asked, looking round.

Carlos brushed her question aside rather abruptly. 'I'll explain later,' he said.

He turned to the man who had addressed him when they had first come into the room. 'The only honest way I could fulfil my function here and make this recording would be to change my name to El Principe.' His voice was rich with irony. 'I think I should never be able to play again.'

'Nonsense,' broke in Elena. '*El pueblo* will never begrudge you money honestly earned by the richness of your own artistry. And whether you want it or not, or whether you now have it or not, you are going to have it three-fold soon. Don't you realise when you make this recording——'

'If! If!' broke in the manager gloomily.

'When——' said Elena emphatically, 'when you make it, you're going to be rich in your own right?'

'They'll say I've only got to the top because of my family connections,' said Carlos, beginning to capitulate in the face of the silent opposition from the group.

'Nonsense!' repeated Elena. 'Moreover,' she went on, sweeping the room with her dark eyes, 'you owe it to these people. Without them you would probably be still begging to be allowed to play in pavement cafés.'

Carlos ran his hand through his hair in the now familiar gesture of exasperation. He turned to Vinny. 'You may have gathered this is a business conference of sorts. When I came back here, penniless, from South America, determined to make myself a success in my own right, I thought things would be simple. Unhappily, my father died the previous year, and having changed his mind about me at the last minute, split his banking empire between Elena and myself. I want to give my half back to her as she's been running the whole show for so long, but the absurd woman won't hear of it. Now we, I and the group, have been offered a recording contract. But how can I, with all this dreadful money, disport myself in front of the people in the guise of a penniless, itinerant musician? The whole thing reeks of hypocrisy.'

'If you have such a fanatical abhorrence of wealth,' laughed Elena, 'you can always give away every single peseta. There are enough charities waiting with open offertory boxes.' She smiled at Vinny, then gave Carlos a searching glance. 'Of course, if you ever decide to marry, you can hardly go empty-handed to your future bride. Have you thought of that?'

Carlos was silent for a moment, then he gave one look at Elena before walking over to the desk where the papers were spread. 'Find me the contract,' he said to one of the men.

Cries of relief broke out from the two dancers and Ribero murmured an ironic *'Olé!'* and snapped his fingers.

'I knew you would eventually be sensible, *caro,*' beamed Elena. 'Now I suggest we all break for a drink, yes?'

Carlos and Vinny were walking slowly through the twilight up the hill to the Alhambra. His arms were tight around her waist and every few yards he would stop and kiss her slowly on the lips.

They hadn't been able to have the promised late-night glass of *ponche* in El Suizo's when, after some time in the recording studios, Carlos had returned to Granada at last.

'I tried to have a cup of coffee there this morning, but I was mobbed. It was impossible. Are you going to mind that sort of thing, my darling?'

In answer Vinny had merely kissed him.

She had falteringly explained to him the reason for her strange behaviour in the chapel of Santa Maria la Blanca, telling him also of her despair when she had seen him outside Curro's with Elena in his arms.

He told her that Elena had just heard of his return to Spain and had come in search of him to let him know of his father's death and his own subsequent change of fortune. He had been so stunned by the news that he had momentarily forgotten everything, and only later, when he returned to the club for his things, had he realised that Vinny had already left. It had somehow seemed too difficult a thing to explain while on tour and he had hoped to be able to see her soon enough to explain the new situation to her face to face.

After saying all this he had looked thoughtful.

'Tell me, *cara*, why were you so wary of me at the beginning?' He paused. His voice was soft when he went on. 'Your eyes seemed to tell me that you loved me, but you wouldn't let me near you.'

Vinny bit her lip and her eyes were moist when she looked up at him. 'I thought some pretty dreadful things about you,' she faltered. 'I don't know how I could—knowing even the little I knew about you then.' She clung to him without being able to speak for a moment, but the warmth of concern showing in his face gave her strength and she said: 'It was because of what happened before we met. . . .'

With a little shudder at the thought of how close to losing him she had been she told him briefly about Zak.

Carlos registered anger for a moment, but without saying anything he pulled her close.

'I'm so sorry,' she whispered as he cradled her in his arms. 'Can you forgive me?'

'I guess I gave you cause for some suspicions,' he smiled rakishly. 'But my disreputable days are gone. Can you forgive *me*, *cara*, for giving you even the shadow of a possibility for doubting me?'

In answer she surrendered her lips to his searching need, and it was some time later that he murmured, 'Are you now beginning to believe in fate a little?' Then he added with a wry smile, 'So many misunderstandings are not natural. Perhaps we should have lit a candle for you on your first day in Granada?'

It was later that they chose a quiet church together on the Hill of Sacromonte and stood for a moment before the bright little flame that flared up, then together they made their way slowly out of the ancient church and started to wend their way up the hill towards the Alhambra.

From the darkening woodland clothing the lower slopes came the sudden liquid sound of a nightingale. It filled the night with its magical beauty.

Vinny was blissful as she looked up at Carlos's strong profile. His glance lifted from her face as his eyes searched the foliage for a glimpse of the bird. It rewarded them with another powerful burst of melody.

'And you are also the Marqués now,' murmured Vinny as the sound died away. 'It will take me some time to get used to that.'

'Don't try,' he told her huskily, drawing her close to him again. 'Know me always as El Brasiliano, or Carlos, the man who loves you.'

He held her close. 'Are you going to mind, my darling, that I am now so horribly famous, not to say rich?'

She smiled up at him.

'I remember what you once said to me—that we'll do as the peasants do. We'll live on love and roses.' As his lips came down on hers she whispered, 'Who cares about fame?'

And, with a new moon rising like a silver sickle in the midnight blue of the sky, they resumed their slow journey towards the palace on the summit of the hill.

THE MUSIC OF THE GYPSIES

In a small Spanish café a guitarist begins to strum. The crowded room is filled with great excitement and anticipation. A man in high-waisted skintight pants and a billowing shirt begins to sing a hoarse but melodic tune. He is joined by a woman, one arm held high over her head, the other at her waist, holding up a corner of her ruffled red dress. The hand in the air makes a slight movement, and the audience cheers to the clack of the castanets. Suddenly she is a blaze of movement and color. Her feet stamp out a beat to the quickening melodies of the guitar, and she punctuates her movements with the clack of castanets and sharp shouts of exhilaration, called *jaleo.*

For this is a *café cantante,* or singing café, in Triana, the Gypsy quarter of the ancient city of Seville. The singers, dancers and guitarists who gather here with *aficionados,* or flamenco fans, are called a *cuadro flamenco.* The *cuadro* performs most of the evening, each member taking a solo turn at dancing or singing while the others provide the instrumental accompaniment.

Flamenco music and dance may be enjoyed anywhere in Spain, but to experience it in Triana is to be close to its historical origins. For while the beginnings of the flamenco are shrouded in mystery, it *is* known that the Gypsies of Seville have been performing it for several hundred years. Until this century, flamenco was the music of the poor, mirroring in song the sad plight of their existence, but through dance bringing color and joy to their lives.

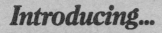